Victoria Benedictsson

VICTORIA BENEDICTSSON (1850-1888), who wrote under the pseudonym Ernst Ahlgren, played a significant role in steering Swedish prose fiction towards greater realism. She grew up in Skåne as the daughter of a gentleman farmer, but she also came into daily contact with farm employees and local folk, and began to write humorous and colourful prose sketches of country life. She wanted to study to be a painter, but her father was near bankruptcy and could not afford to send her to Stockholm. At the age of 21 she accepted a marriage proposal from a local postmaster, a prosperous widower of 48 with several children. She later had two daughters of her own, one of whom lived only a few weeks. She increasingly took leave from her domestic responsibilities, travelling to Copenhagen to attend lectures by radical literary figures like Georg Brandes; and to Malmö for treatment for a persistent leg problem. She wrote prolifically, often in collaboration with fellow author Axel Lundegård, though his editing of her work after her death has now been shown to be of dubious merit and motivation. Over many years she kept a diary, known as *Stora boken*, which with her letters provides great insights into her mind and working methods. After completing *Pengar* (*Money*) in 1885, she went to stay in Stockholm, where she moved in literary circles and became friends with Ellen Key. She produced many short stories, one-act plays and monologues, and in 1887 wrote her second novel, *Fru Marianne* (Mistress Marianne), in which she sought to show a woman finding fulfilment within marriage.

SARAH DEATH has translated works in many genres and from a variety of periods of Swedish literature, by writers including Fredrika Bremer, Selma Lagerlöf, Astrid Lindgren, Sven Lindqvist, Steve Sem-Sandberg and Elin Wägner. She has twice won the George Bernard Shaw Prize for translation from Swedish, for Kerstin Ekman's *The Angel House* (Norvik Press) and Ellen Mattson's *Snow* (Jonathan Cape). She is the editor of the journal *Swedish Book Review*.

Some other books from Norvik Press

Kjell Askildsen: *A Sudden Liberating Thought* (translated by Sverre Lyngstad)

Hjalmar Bergman: *Memoirs of a Dead Man* (translated by Neil Smith)

Jens Bjørneboe: *Moment of Freedom* (translated by Esther Greenleaf Mürer)

Jens Bjørneboe: *Powderhouse* (translated by Esther Greenleaf Mürer)

Jens Bjørneboe: *The Silence* (translated by Esther Greenleaf Mürer)

Johan Borgen: *The Scapegoat* (translated by Elizabeth Rokkan)

Fredrika Bremer: *The Colonel's Family* (translated by Sarah Death)

Kerstin Ekman: *Witches' Rings* (translated by Linda Schenck)

Kerstin Ekman: *The Spring* (translated by Linda Schenck)

Kerstin Ekman: *The Angel House* (translated by Sarah Death)

Kerstin Ekman: *City of Light* (translated by Linda Schenck)

Arne Garborg: *Tha Making of Daniel Braut* (translated by Marie Wells)

P. C. Jersild: *A Living Soul* (translated by Rika Lesser)

Selma Lagerlöf: *Lord Arne's Silver* (translated by Sarah Death) (2011)

Selma Lagerlöf: *The Löwensköld Ring* (translated by Linda Schenck) (2011)

Selma Lagerlöf: *The Phantom Carriage* (translated by Peter Graves) (2011)

Viivi Luik: *The Beauty of History* (translated by Hildi Hawkins)

Henry Parland: *To Pieces* (translated by Dinah Cannell) (2011)

Amalie Skram: *Lucie* (translated by Katherine Hanson and Judith Messick)

Amalie and Erik Skram: *Caught in the Enchanter's Net: Selected Letters* (edited and translated by Janet Garton)

August Strindberg: *Tschandala* (translated by Peter Graves)

August Strindberg: *The Red Room* (translated by Peter Graves)

Hanne Marie Svendsen: *Under the Sun* (translated by Marina Allemano)

Hjalmar Söderberg: *Martin Birck's Youth* (translated by Tom Ellett)

Hjalmar Söderberg: *Selected Stories* (translated by Carl Lofmark)

Anton Tammsaare: *The Misadventures of the New Satan* (translated by Olga Shartze and Christopher Moseley)

Ellen Wägner: *Penwoman* (translated by Sarah Death)

2

MONEY

by

Victoria Benedictsson

Translated from the Swedish
and with an afterword
by

Sarah Death

Norvik Press
2011

Originally published in Swedish by Bonniers Förlag under the title
Pengar (1885).

This translation and afterword © Sarah Death 2011
The translator's moral right to be identified as the translator of the work
has been asserted.

A catalogue record for this book is available from the British Library.

ISBN: 978-1-870041-85-0

First published in 1999 by Norvik Press. This revised edition first
published in 2011.

Norvik Press gratefully acknowledges the financial assistance of The
Swedish Institute towards the publication of the first edition of this
translation.

Norvik Press
Department of Scandinavian Studies
University College London
Gower Street
London WC1E 6BT
United Kingdom

Website: www.norvikpress.com
E-mail address: norvik.press@ucl.ac.uk

Managing editors: Sarah Death, Helena Forsås-Scott, Janet Garton, C.
Claire Thomson.

Cover illustration: Based on a paper silhouette made by Victoria
Benedictsson, who took up paper cutting in the early 1880s. Her
silhouette album is preserved in the Ernst Ahlgren Archive at Lund
University Library.

Cover design: Richard Johnson
Layout: Elettra Carbone

Printed in the UK by Lightning Source UK Ltd.

Contents

Chapter 1

The village comprised no more than a single street, if indeed it could be considered worthy even of that name, since it was quite simply a dirt track, inexcusably poorly maintained. Down one side was a row of five or six inferior houses, on the other a number of farmhouses, some distance apart, with room for quite large gardens between them. These farms might be respectable enough, with their broad buildings grouped round square, regular courtyards, but to anyone walking along the road they looked singularly unfriendly, as they had all turned their backs, having only their outbuildings at the front. There was only one place where a door had been left open, affording a view of a courtyard, in which no living creature could be seen but a family of hens, scratching in the hay.

It had been a cold and rainy summer, and now even that was over.

With her hands thrust into the pockets of her outgrown overcoat, a young woman came walking down the street. She looked happy and lively; her gait had nothing of the mincing charm of a lady from town, but rather the gangling action of an adolescent boy. She studied the grey clouds in the sky with a carefree air, to see if it was going to rain again. Then she opened the door to one of the low houses and stepped into the hallway, which was just big enough for the doors to clear each other. She opened the inner door too, to the furious jangling of a doorbell.

This was the only general store in the village, the only place to buy tobacco, coffee and sugar. And a poky little hole it was – low-ceilinged, dark and smoky – and with that indescribable smell of coarse grey paper, soap, and all the rest!

A young man stood behind the counter with his elbows resting on it and his head bent over a book. His appearance was as light and amiable as the shop's was dark and disagreeable.

As the young woman entered, he straightened up and bowed. He was quite good-looking. His blonde hair was wavy, shiny as silk and smoothed well back. His skin was as fair as a woman's, and there could never be a pair of eyes bluer than his. A degree of intelligence glittered behind those spectacles, but there was a cowed look about his expression, and there were lines of vulnerability around the mouth, which with only the slightest shift would turn to melancholy. There was nothing lively, nothing manly about him; he was like one of those plants which produce white rather than green leaves through lack of light.

No-one was ever likely to say an unkind word to Axel Möller. There was that indefinable something about his look and attitude that always seemed to be apologizing. One felt an involuntary sense of pity – and yet he was neither sick, nor old, nor poor.

Even Selma Berg's boyish manner was somewhat muted when she addressed him.

'I haven't come to buy anything,' she said, coming up to the counter, 'but to ask you something.'

'Me?' he asked happily, a slight flush colouring his cheeks.

She felt awkward. It was true that they had met a few times at the rectory, but what she was doing now was undoubtedly terribly forward. His shyness communicated itself to her, and her fingers played nervously with the loose end of the reel of twine.

'Richard told me that your grandfather has lots of drawings and sketches done by your uncle.'

A glittering behind the spectacles; a sort of silent assent.

'I wanted to ... oh, I would be so grateful if you could ask your grandfather ... It would make me so terribly happy, if I could see them.'

The young man was silent and seemed to be hesitating.

Selma blushed so much that tears came into her eyes. She really had been dreadfully presumptuous.

'Or don't you think that your grandfather ... ?'

'Grandfather, oh yes. He likes nothing better than showing all those things.' He considered for a moment.

'I shall go in and tell Mother,' he said briskly.

He went into the living room at the back and returned after a few moments.

'Please come in,' he said, holding the door open.

Selma complied, stepping into a large living room, with little windows on both sides. Old Mother Möller and her daughter sat at one of them, sewing.

Selma had only seen the old lady at church, but that face with its pointed nose, once seen, was not forgotten.

Her son made the introductions and the young woman uttered some words of apology for her boldness. These were received with a rather forced politeness, but Selma did not let this worry her. She knew about Old Mother Möller, as one knows everyone in such a small village, and she knew that the old woman was habitually less than amiable. Besides, what was the old crone to her? So she thrust her hands into her coat pockets and assumed a real street-urchin expression. That was her usual tactic when anyone treated her in a less than friendly manner.

Her curious gaze flitted around the room and fell on a little picture, hanging above a bureau. It was as well to take a look round now; there were unlikely to be any further visits.

'Did your uncle paint that?' she asked the young man. But before he could reply, his mother interjected:

'No, Axel did it. When he was a child, he dabbled in things like that.'

'Do you plan to become an artist?'

'No he does not. We have had one artist in the family, and that was more than enough.'

'It's very good. Mr Möller, you have certainly inherited your uncle's talent.'

'That is all he has inherited from him, and scarcely worth having. Money was spent like water on him, and when he died, he left nothing behind him but debts.'

'But just think – to make such a name.'

'I can tell you young lady, there is no living to be made from that.'

Old Mother Möller pursed her lips in a manner which irreparably severed the thread of the conversation.

Selma threw the young man a look. He understood her.

'Grandfather's room is out here; may I ask you to come this way?'

With a word of farewell to her hostess, Selma left the room, and breathed a sigh of relief once her companion had shut the door after them.

They went through a drawing room – formal, tasteless, symmetrical. The mere sight of it was enough to make one shiver.

The next room had a completely different character.

'This is mine,' said Mr Möller.

Selma looked about her. She had that alert eye which assimilates everything, down to the last detail.

It was a shabby room, but it looked lived in. One could sit there for hours on end and still not feel alone, so thoroughly had the owner's taste set its stamp on everything.

'You read a lot,' said the guest, looking about her.

'Every spare moment.'

'What sort of thing?' she asked, as she studied the spines of a few volumes that had come from a rural book auction. 'Ah, novels! Do you read anything else?'

'Yes, poetry; I like that best, and then history. Do you never read novels, Miss Berg?'

'Yes, of course, but I read philosophy and physics too.'

Her inimitable tone was altogether lost on him; he was far too naive to laugh. On the contrary, he felt something akin to admiration.

'Isn't that difficult?' he asked timidly.

'It depends how you approach it,' she answered casually. She felt increasingly aware of her superiority.

'Do you play the violin?'

'Yes, occasionally.'

'Who taught you?'

'I taught myself, Mother has never liked spending money on me.'

'And that little pianino, is that yours too?'

'Yes, but it is very poor, I wish I could afford to buy a new one.'

'Afford to?' she echoed. After all, everyone knew that Old Mother Möller was rich.

'Yes, afford to,' he repeated with a smile.

She nodded knowingly to herself, as if to say, 'Now I understand.'

The room was full of tempting objects, all those things that would delight a schoolboy 'collector'. Moss and stones, big snails, flint arrowheads and – best of all! – a little aquarium of a primitive design, containing watersnakes and lizards. But it was not proper to linger there any longer, and they went on.

They reached the old man's room via a little corridor or hall.

'Grandfather, Miss Berg is asking to see Uncle's drawings,' said her companion as he entered and held open the door for her.

His voice had a tone quite different from that of a moment before.

The old man was sitting in the armchair at his desk, reading. He rose and pushed his spectacles up onto his forehead. It was remarkable how closely his nephew resembled him, but the old man had a more vital look.

'Welcome,' he said warmly, and extended his hand to her.

'This is very presumptuous of me,' she said, looking the old man straight in the eye, 'but there's nothing I enjoy better than drawing and sketching; I'm quite mad about it ... and since I knew that there was so much to see here ... The temptation was too great.' She burst into an unprovoked little peal of laughter. It was a refreshing sound, and the old man liked her for it.

Axel stood in the middle of the floor, shifting his weight from one foot to the other; he appeared to be enjoying himself.

'How kind, how very kind,' said the old man, and patted her confidingly on the shoulder, as if they had been old acquaintances.

His nephew looked around him with apparent pleasure, although all this must be so utterly familiar to him.

Suddenly he said, 'Miss Berg, what do you think?' He indicated a lithograph, which hung opposite the window, above

11

the bed.

The young girl stared sat it, transfixed. It was the idea behind the picture that appealed to her – she who still lived half in childhood fairyland. There it was, as large as life, with beautiful fairytale creatures, as romantic and enchanting as a summer night. Just the thing for her!

Axel Möller was ready to hold his breath, he was so afraid of disturbing her.

Here in his grandfather's room they had germinated, all those seeds which nature had planted in his mind, here they had grown shoots without air, without light – sickly and distorted – and here he had entered into the old man's worship of the departed uncle. It seemed to him as though the artist's spirit still lingered here, and as she stood in silent admiration, it was to his deity that she did obeisance.

The combination of being shut off from the world and treated harshly by his mother had caused his willpower to shrink from childhood to the stature of a dwarf, whilst his imagination flourished until it would have filled the head of a giant. He was one of those people who believe themselves born to suffer, just because they have the ability to surrender to a sentiment.

'Oh, how enchanting!' cried Selma, splaying out her fingers inside her coat pockets.

Another reverent silence followed.

Her audience had no sense of the ridiculous, and were oblivious to the contrast between the fully-perfected enthusiasm of the young lady and that genuinely awkward adolescent manner.

'And what about these?' she said, including in her gesture all the other pictures on the walls. She couldn't just stand there admiring forever, could she now?

'All copies of his work. He always used to send them home to me. And this oil painting is a study from life that he did himself,' said the old man with pride.

It was a picture of a nude figure with an ugly head, skilfully done. Ugh, how horrid! thought Selma in her girls' boarding school fashion, but she said nothing.

'It's getting so dark. May I light your lamp, Grandfather?' said Axel.

'How silly of me to come so late!' moaned Selma, 'But it's all because I walked up and down the road for an hour, wondering whether I dared to or not.'

That made them laugh, and then the ice was broken; she could sense that she was their favourite now.

'May I take off my coat?' she asked. And the old man helped her himself, while his nephew lit the lamp and let down the blind.

It was as if this was just what the old furniture had needed. It no longer looked stiff and angular. Everything went together so well; it was full of old memories and old stories. You felt so much at home in this room!

The young man adjusted his grandfather's chair and offered their guest a seat there. The happy expression improved his looks; he looked more vigorous than usual.

'Do you want to get out the portfolios now, Grandfather?'

The old man opened the desk and began bringing out his treasures. Selma leapt forward and sat down in the armchair. You could be so free with these people!

She craned over the back of her chair to see the room behind her. The lamplight fell sideways onto her upturned face and clearly illuminated her pert, immature figure. She was not beautiful, rather the opposite, but she had a freshness reminiscent of a cloudless winter day with snow and sleighbells.

This room appealed to her. There was nothing half-hearted, it was entirely what it was. With indescribable satisfaction she allowed her gaze to travel around the walls and shelves. There were things tucked in everywhere: no space was left empty. And everything was so dark, it really seemed to soak up the light from the lamp. And think what fun it would be to rummage around in all those cupboards and drawers! She gave a laugh.

'It's so very nice here!'

Her delight was reflected in the young man's face. He stood looking at her.

'Here we are,' said the old man, putting a pile of pictures on the table. Then he drew a chair up beside hers, so he could explain everything; and his nephew stood behind them, where he could look over her shoulder.

She was so interested – scrutinizing and asking questions. As she did so, she looked so trustingly into the old man's face that his reticence melted and he grew frank and talkative. As they went through the contents of the portfolios he talked about his son, who had been the pride and joy of his life.

'You see, Miss, I was a simple house-painter,' he said, 'but let me tell you I knew my job. He had the basic principles from me, and – you see, Miss – that stood him in good stead ever after.'

This was the old man's inexhaustible source of joy, the fact that he had given him 'the basic principles'. That was his gospel, and he would hold fast to it, even if all else crumbled.

'And it cost me, Miss, I can tell you. First to keep him at school in Lund – because he had to work hard at his studies, of course. Because if you're going to be an artist, see, it's not enough just to daub on the colour, you have to learn this, that and the other – and then in Stockholm at the Academy. But I was a hard worker, and I couldn't have been happier than when I was working for my boy. Sara, she resented it of course – but no-one need pay any heed to that.'

Sara, that was Old Mother Möller.

Axel gave the old man's shoulder a quick squeeze. He did not think that last utterance quite proper. Miss Berg was a well-brought-up lady, after all, and Grandfather should preserve his dignity.

Selma glanced up and smiled, with a look that seemed to say: let him go on.

'The Baron was always very decent,' went on the old man, 'and helped him all the time, whenever things were difficult.'

As far as the old house-painter was concerned, there was only one baron in the world, and that was the one on whose estate he had been employed.

And so he continued his story.

Selma had that way of listening, with her whole and undivided attention, which makes such a pleasant impact on whoever is speaking, and her thoughtful little expression was as effective as any refined flattery.

Everything seemed to her so immeasurably interesting – the room, the people, the story.

Now she had forgotten the fantastical painting over there, with its moonlight and water sprite.

And all this time, the young man stood behind her chair and took pleasure in the happiness and sense of well-being she had brought with her. For him she was something utterly out of the ordinary, for his mother's house was seldom visited by women other than old country wives, or the occasional rich tenant farmer's daughter coming to see his sister, and trying to appear so well-bred and superior that she could scarcely speak or move like an ordinary human being. With a mixture of peasant pride and self-importance born of her money, Old Mother Möller detested all that 'people of rank' stood for, and in spite of much pleading she would not be persuaded to allow her daughter to wear a hat. A headscarf it was.

It was growing late, but Selma did not seem to notice. There was still so much here to ask about and to find out. This pleased her two hosts, and at the same time they felt a little anxious, as we might be when a little bird comes hopping into the room, and we are frightened of making a single movement to remind him that he is in the wrong place. It is such a splendid thing to see him so confident and at ease, and yet we know he may fly away at any moment.

Sometimes, when she found a drawing she liked better than the others, she threw herself back in her seat and looked up into the young man's face, to see if he shared her admiration. As she did this, she always met his gaze, smiling at her, albeit with a certain melancholy.

And he saw her with the light full on her face.

She had a broad, white forehead, with straw-coloured hair falling over it in a straggling fringe; her nose was small and of a comical design, her complexion the freshest one could possibly imagine, and her thin lips were such a bright red that they looked painted. But perhaps they appeared so by contrast with the whiteness of her chin. The lower part of her face was as sharp and pointed as the upper part was broad and firm. This gave her a strangely determined look, and made her ugly at the same time.

'Oh, how late it is, and dark, as well!' she cried, and jumped up so suddenly that her chair knocked into Axel.

'Whatever can the time be?' She turned her head in all directions to find the clock. 'Half past seven! Uncle and Aunt will be really cross with me; I won't be home in time for supper.'

She rushed over to the bed, where her coat was lying, and pulled it on in a single movement.

'Thank you so very much for such a nice time,' she said, shaking hands with the old man whilst deftly pinning on her hat with the other hand. 'But – oh, if only I were home!'

'I shall come with you, Miss,' said Axel.

'Yes, that is all very well. But – what trouble I shall be in!'

Axel opened the door.

'Is there any other way out than through your mother's room?' she said quickly.

'Yes, through this hall,' he replied, feeling relief himself as he did so.

They emerged into the little village street. It was dark, and drizzly rain greeted them.

'Wait a minute, I'll run and fetch Grandfather's umbrella.'

He ran in and was immediately back again, so they set off. She walked close beside him, as he was holding the umbrella.

'Shall we take the short cut by the railway embankment?' he asked.

'Yes,' she answered. And then they were silent for a time.

When they reached the gate, he opened it, and they went onto the smooth railway, between the tracks, where the ground had been stamped and compacted by the lengthsmen's steps.

'Won't you be able to walk more easily if you take my arm?' he asked.

She considered for a moment whether it would be proper, and then took his arm.

The rain pattered hard on the umbrella in the stiff breeze. They matched their steps to each other.

'It's instructive to hear how other people have made a career for themselves,' she said.

'I find it depressing.'

'Why?'

'I see everyone making their way in the world except me.'

'Why not you?'

'Because it's too late now.'

'But why couldn't you have done it before?'

'Money, money! Mother cares for nothing in the world but money. I didn't realize it before, but now I do.'

She was gripping his arm more tightly than at first, and their mutual shyness had vanished. She saw that he wanted to talk to her as a wise, mature person. That was almost a mission for her to undertake!

'Tell me,' she said quickly.

'What?'

'Everything. Don't you think I can keep quiet?'

'There's nothing to tell; nothing that anyone would find entertaining.'

'Entertaining!' she burst out contemptuously. As if she hadn't long since grown out of being entertained! Hmm.

The conversation briefly stalled. Now she was offended.

He saw it.

'Could it be of any interest to you, Miss?' he said hesitantly and somewhat weakly.

'Come, come!' she said emphatically, and pulled on his arm for a little. That was what she did, when one of her schoolfriends wanted to unburden herself, but did not seem able to.

'Oh Miss, if my sister were the least like you!'

'What is she like, then?'

'She doesn't care about anything – not a single thing – and I feel so terribly alone.'

'But you have your grandfather.'

'He's so old, though.'

'And you have my cousin Richard.'

'We're so different. He's at university, and here am I trapped between the counter and the snuff barrel.'

'And you have me. What is it? Tell me!'

He was silent for a moment; she had uttered words that he wanted to repeat to himself. His voice had altered when he replied; there was suppressed emotion in it.

'Miss, I can't even speak. I have never had anyone to speak to.'

She said nothing. A woman's instinct told her that he just needed time.

'They haven't treated me fairly,' he began. 'I'm nothing, I know nothing, and everything I try to do turns out wrong. I can't even sell herring and salt properly. I'm no good at singing the praises of my wares. All that is hateful to me. And now I'm sick of it.'

'But then why not be something else?'

'Mother doesn't want me to.'

'Why?'

'She says I can take over the shop; that's enough to live on.'

'Well?'

'Can I stand it in that black hole day after day?'

'Then why don't you go somewhere else?'

'Where would I get the money? And how far would I get without a sound knowledge of anything, without recommendations? If I were bound hand and foot, it couldn't be any worse.'

'But you are of age?'

'What good is that, when there is nothing to be of age for?'

'Have you no paternal inheritance?'

That made her sound a horrible know-all, but he didn't notice. Such things were always lost on him.

'No, I have nothing. Father died when we were very young, and there wasn't anything. Mother set up the shop herself and scraped it all together.'

'But she's rich, isn't she?'

'Yes, they say so.'

'But – I know – since she started with nothing, why can't you do the same?'

This question silenced him for a moment.

'Ah, Miss – it's not so easy to put into practice.'

'Hm – well anyway, I shall be forced to earn some money, that's for certain.'

'Why?'

'My father is getting poorer and poorer; soon he will have nothing to give me. Things are going backwards.'

This last was said in such an indescribably comical manner – as if that were the final word, as if it were quite natural for things to be 'going backwards'. An indisputable fact and that was that.

'What will you do?' he asked, as interested as if he had struck gold.

'Well, I don't really know, but I must have money. You see, I want to be an artist – to paint animals, I'm sure of that – but of course I dare not tell anyone yet, because it costs such a lot. I must find the money first.'

'But how will you do that?'

'Ah, I have my plans, you see. And then perhaps one might find somebody.'

'What?'

'Somebody who could help, like that baron helped your uncle.'

He was silent. He felt stung to the heart. If that happened? Then she would go away – perhaps make a name for herself – and he would stay behind, alone.

'What if you were to be a painter too, and we were friends and companions!'

Her cry was so sudden and so youthfully exuberant. It was a gust of wind which reawakened all the ideas he had from novels, so they began circling round each other in his brain – castles in the air, illusions – all in a moment. Her for a friend and companion! ... Once again he saw her leaning over the back of the chair, with the light full on her face. Her for a companion, and freedom ... freedom!

He had to stop for a moment.

'What is it?'

'Dear God – yes,' he said, taking a deep breath.

And they continued on their way. But their thoughts were

running along new lines. They were all dreams of the future, half in jest, half serious. All at once they had found common interests, common successes and common enemies. Oblivious to the rain and their surroundings, they went a good way past the gate, through which they should have turned off to the rectory.

They had to retrace their steps.

He gave a deep sigh as they stood at the gate, with only a few steps remaining before they were to part.

'Something will turn up,' she said, 'That's my motto.'

'Mottos never come true,' he remarked gloomily.

For a while they walked in silence along the road.

'Just think if a train had come along: that would have been our last walk,' he said. 'I really doubt we would have heard it in this weather.'

He found a certain satisfaction in saying this.

Selma made no reply; she was thinking of the scolding that awaited her. They found themselves at the garden gate.

'Good night,' she said, holding out her hand.

It would never have occurred to him to squeeze it more warmly.

Thus they parted.

Once Selma had removed her outdoor things, she went into the family sitting-room. Her uncle lay on the sofa reading a newspaper, his wife sat beside him knitting stockings. Selma's practised eye immediately detected that supper was over.

'Please excuse me for coming in so late, Aunt,' she said cordially, though far from humbly. 'I went in to Old Mother Möller's father to see all the drawings he has, and I didn't notice the time. I was really cross with myself.'

Her uncle was evidently angry, for he made no answer and did not look up from his paper, although it was obvious that he was not reading it.

'How did you get home, young lady?', said her aunt.

'I walked, of course,' replied Selma, resenting the sour looks.

'Alone?'

'No, Mr Möller came with me.'

'But let me tell you that it is not at all proper to go running around the village with gentlemen at this time of day.'

'But I didn't go running around with him.'

'I will have no impertinence from you!' bellowed the Rector, looking up.

'God forbid – Uncle,' she said, giving him a rather mischievous look, which she could use to perfection when it was needed.

'Do not take God's name in vain. I thought I had made myself clear on that point already.'

She looked at him with a disarmingly roguish expression, which seemed to say: I shall keep quiet – since I can't talk you round, Uncle dear.

He turned back to his newspaper, as he was finding it difficult to look stern, although he wanted to. He had been so angry throughout the meal that he had felt the rage really boiling inside him. But now that she was standing there so red and white and cheerful, he was unable to muster a single word of all that he had wanted to say.

'But let me tell you, young lady,' began her aunt in a lecturing tone – she always called her that when she was cross – 'that I would go so far as to say that it is highly improper to allow oneself to be brought home by young gentlemen, when one is only your age, young lady. No less than a rendezvous, a private conversation! Well that would not have done in my young days, I must say. No, we were obliged to behave properly.'

'But I assure you, Aunt, that we only said what the whole world ...' – could have heard, she had meant to say, but she had a scrupulous love of the truth, which made her pause – 'that is to say, we only talked business,' she added.

'Business?' echoed Mrs Berg with an astonishment bordering on horror, 'Did he talk to you about his business affairs?'

'Yes, he did. And I talked to him about mine too; what's wrong with that?'

'What do you mean, your business affairs?' asked her uncle in his driest tone.

She took a step forward, driven by a burning urge to act, to change things. This was a highly enterprising and intrepid woman.

21

'I mean that I think I would like to earn some money.'

'Oh, is that what you would like?' he answered in a respectful tone with just a hint of a sneer. 'And how would that be arranged, if I may ask? Perhaps you would become Mr Möller's associate?'

She was so filled with her plans that she had no time to consider what might lie behind his words.

'Well Uncle, you know that what I was better at than all my friends at the boarding school was drawing, and so I thought it would be best to take up something along those lines.'

'I se-ee.'

'Yes. And so I thought that perhaps you, Uncle, might help me to get into the College of Art and Design in Stockholm. You can learn lots of practical things there can be useful for earning money. I mean, I can't rely on Papa.'

'No-o. You're right there, God help you!'

'But anyway Uncle, would it be such a bad idea?'

'We'll have to see. But that would cost a good deal of money too, I can tell you.'

'Yes, it really is true that you can't get anywhere without money!' she exclaimed with a worried frown. 'But couldn't I take out a life insurance policy?'

'My child,' he said severely, 'where did you get all that silly nonsense from?'

She looked down and stuck out her lip, shamefaced, but did not answer. She had learnt all these misplaced business terms in her father's company. They would keep on coming out of her mouth, and were always getting her into trouble.

She poked an index finger into one of the buttonholes of her dress, where she twisted and turned it in embarrassment. She knew she was making herself ridiculous by all this, but since that was how it was, then ...

'There's always my inheritance from my mother,' she pointed out, blushing furiously.

'Yes. And roughly how much do you think that might be?' asked her uncle, struggling to keep a straight face.

'Seven hundred and thirty-one kronor and eighty-two öre,' she answered in a low voice, on the verge of tears. She was very sensitive to being laughed at, and knew that he would find it amusing that she knew so exactly. But she could not lie.

'But you are not of age, you cannot get at it!' He fought down his laughter until he felt as if his insides were turning upside down.

'I thought that if one petitioned ...'

Now his amusement broke out, uncontrollably; he roared with laughter.

The blush had spread to her hairline, and she stuck out her lip still further to keep from bursting into tears, but she stood her ground in the circle of light from the lamp. She was a brave woman.

'Well, I shall think about it, perhaps it can be arranged,' her uncle said. Now he felt sorry for her.

'Then I can write to Papa about it?' she said without looking up, and still in a businesslike tone.

'Yes, you can. I shall write this evening as well.'

'But my dear Berg,' said his wife in her elaborate, roundabout way, 'there can naturally be no question of that until later on. One never knows ... that is to say, it is not really a woman's true calling, and these new ideas ... well, I would go so far as to say, that the point actually is, that it is not really right. If older unmarried women resort to such things, all well and good, but at Selma's age there truly are so many other and more necessary things to learn. It is no easy matter to run a household, and any sensible man will always be looking out for a capable girl, I can tell you.'

'But I'm sure that no-one will want me,' protested Selma with grave conviction.

Her uncle coughed. It was an artificial, warning cough.

'You can go in and eat now, young lady,' said her aunt.

Her uncle watched her go, to check that she was out of earshot.

'It might be a good idea, though, not to need to throw oneself away on just any kind of fellow,' he said.

Chapter 2

It was an unusually fine autumn day, and Axel Möller had propped open the doors to the street to let the air and light into the dark shop.

He himself was sitting on a sugar barrel in the far corner, with his back against the wall and his fiddle under his chin.

He was improvising.

There was a singular contrast between the inspired expression on his face and the wretched mishmash he was producing. An artist merely seeing him would have been enchanted; a musician merely hearing would have been in despair. There was nothing more lamentable to be heard than this helpless groping for something he could never capture, those openings of well-known melodies, which were not allowed to develop, because by obscuring them he tried to convince himself that he was composing, and finally those haphazard runs, the fruits of his concert visits. But there was no doubt that he believed himself to be creating something beautiful, and that he took delight in it.

A shadow fell across the doorway. He looked up and saw Selma. Her silhouette was sharply outlined against the sunny background; she had on a dark blue dress, which was close-fitting and made her look even slimmer.

'I would have liked to hear you play, but I dare not because of your mother,' she said laughingly, supporting herself with a hand on each side of the door frame and swinging her body forward as far as her arms would stretch.

His face lit up with pleasure when he saw her, but before he could answer, she was gone.

Even after that, he thought he could hear a stifled laugh and glimpse a row of white teeth over there in the shadows. He put his fiddle on the counter and thought for a moment. It was likely that she would turn off through the gate and walk home along the railway embankment. And in that case ... what a blessing that the overgrown currant bushes obscured the view from his mother's window!

He grabbed his hat from one of the shelves and slipped out, leaving the shop to its fate. Having turned round the side of the building, he walked straight across the field to the railway line.

He arrived before her, as she had to come by a less direct route. It was not worth going to meet her; his mother might be able to see after all. He threw himself down in the grass below the track and waited.

He soon saw her. Her stride was uninhibited and her hands were clasped behind her back. Her head was bent, her gaze fixed on the ground. She appeared to be thinking.

Mr Möller stood up and greeted her.

'Ooh, fancy lying in wait for people!' she said with a laugh.

'Did I frighten you, Miss?'

'Oh no, you don't look so very hideous, and I'm not that timid either.'

He climbed onto the embankment and fell in beside her, but did not know what to say.

She looked at him in profile. He had a nice-looking grey suit and a modern felt hat. She thought that on the whole he looked quite smart, but he did walk with a terrible stoop! And she never could bear spectacles.

'You know, I got straight on with it,' she said in her easy way.

He gave her an enquiring look.

'I mean, I went straight to the old man at home and told him I wanted to go to Stockholm.'

'And?'

'Oh yes, I'm sure it will be all right. I'm just waiting for a letter from my Papa. And he will certainly not say no, now Uncle has said yes; for Papa admires Uncle so frightfully. I'm sure he thinks he'll be made a bishop one of these days!' She laughed.

'Did you get into as much trouble as you thought you would?'

'Oh no, nothing serious. And anyway it's like water off a duck's back; I just shake myself and it's all over. But – by the way – ,' she stopped in front of him with a gesture that suggested she had just remembered something, 'Aunt doesn't think it proper for me to be out walking with you. Do you feel like going back?'

'Pardon?'

'Back to your house.' She waved a hand in the direction of the village and regarded him merrily, revelling in his discomfort and waiting to see what impression her words would make.

He looked embarrassed and did not know how to reply. He wondered whether she really did want him to turn back.

'Because *I* simply have to go home now,' she went on innocently, 'so if you are going the *same way*, I can't see how I can avoid your company.'

Chewing one finger of her glove, she peeped sideways at him.

He flushed self-consciously. There was never any joking in his home, and he had a vague suspicion that she was making fun of him.

'Do you dislike me coming with you, Miss?' he said meekly.

She was touched.

'Ah, you're such a child,' she said in a superior way; 'Surely you could tell that I didn't mean to upset you? How old are you?'

'Twenty-two.'

'Yes, it's awful. I'm not even seventeen yet, and yet it's as if I were older than you. But I suppose that's because ... '

'Because you've read so much,' he hazarded.

'Yes, perhaps that too,' she said dismissively. 'But I meant that it was because I was the one at boarding school who always had to look after the others.'

He did not find it at all remarkable that she had to 'look after' people in that way. Her mysterious learning impressed him. And then, he had never before met a young girl who could talk of having been at 'boarding school'. Only in novels had he read of such things. It all seemed terribly grand to him.

His mother's oppression had made him as excessively unassuming as he was excessively ambitious.

26

They walked in silence for a while.

'So how are they going?' she said finally.

'How are what going?'

'Your plans for the future. Have you spoken to your mother yet?'

'No.'

He looked down, as if he were ashamed.

'You daren't?'

'Oh yes, I dare, but ... '

'No you don't. Do you want ... ' She stopped short and looked at him. 'Do you want me to speak to her?'

'Oh my goodness, no!'

He looked almost frightened.

'Don't you think I've done more than that for my friends?' she said with a proud little smile as they went on.

He hardly knew what to believe: speaking to his mother seemed to him almost the worst thing imaginable.

'And let me tell you, if one doesn't get on with it, nothing will ever be achieved in this world,' she resumed, infinitely wise.

Once more they walked beside one another in silence. He saw with dread how fast they were approaching the gate over by the clump of trees, where she would be turning off. And he had a thousand things to say. If she went away to Stockholm now, they might be parted forever.

He sank into thought.

His mother could surely not live forever. Then he would be free, and half her fortune would be his. Just think if she were prepared to wait for him! But it never occurred to him to ask.

He only looked at her, and asked a distrustful question:

'Your career as an artist is not likely to last very long, is it?' he said in a low voice. 'Suddenly, one of these days, you'll go and get married.'

'I don't think I am ever likely to marry,' she answered gravely, 'That's precisely why I want to work.'

To him, this seemed almost a promise, which sent him into silent ecstasy.

She, too, was silent.

'How amusing it would be to meet when we were old,' she said suddenly, looking up.

Radiant with happiness, he met her gaze; he felt like ... no, he did not dare.

Now they were at the gate. She opened it for herself, slipped lightly through, and let it slam shut. He was left on the far side.

She rested her arms on top of the gate and looked him mischievously straight in the eye.

'Let's agree that we will both be successful in our different fields. What does it matter if you become a painter or anything else, as long as you have spirit and you reach your goal. Are you with me?'

With great resolve she held out her hand in its worn glove.

'Let's shake on it, I can guarantee my part,' she went on gaily, 'and then we'll meet when we're old.' She stuck her thumb in the air.

He stood looking at the headstrong young woman hanging over the gate, but he did not accept her challenge and drew back his hand.

'You'll be a success,' he said, 'but I won't.'

'Is it always money, money?' she said, smiling.

'Yes,' he said quickly, 'But there is no-one in the whole world I like better than ... '

He flushed at his own boldness.

'Nonsense! *I* like everyone; including you,' she said cheerfully. 'Shake hands with me on that, at least.'

She extended her hand to him over the gate, and he took it – lamely, as if he were afraid of it. Then she jumped down and walked quickly away, without looking round.

The letter from her father could certainly have come by now. She approached the front of the house.

At the foot of the steps stood an elegant phaeton drawn by two greys. She knew them well. They belonged to Squire Kristerson. How beautiful they were! She could not help stroking them before she went up the steps.

On reaching the drawing room, she found no-one there. So the Squire was downstairs with Uncle? Well in that case, she didn't feel like going to ask about the letter.

Instead she went to the dining room to see if there was any coffee to be had, but it was all gone. She opened one of the windows, knelt on a chair and rested her elbows on the window-frame to get a better view of the horses. A position that was more comfortable than graceful.

What in the world could the Squire be doing with Uncle all this time? Generally he would come up to the drawing room to play chess with her. And they were always sure to fall out. She wondered whether this time he was genuinely annoyed, because she had taken his queen so craftily in their last game. It was certainly true that he had not been there since. But why in the world should that worry him, he had checkmated her, after all.

Fine horses! Must be fun to ride behind them! How splendid it looked as they nodded, making all the little silver mirrors between their ears sparkle in the sun!

It was true that she had not met the Squire since that evening at the doctor's house. He had danced three dances with her. He – who was usually so lazy!

She laughed at the thought.

He danced well, at any rate, and led so firmly. But what had he been thinking of? Every time he turned at the end of the room, he had put his arm more tightly round her, so she was forced right up against him.

She blushed now, remembering it. Wonder if he always does that? The other girls said that he danced so well, they had made insinuations about the three dances. But then, she had been wearing her new dress, the one with the satin trim, that was so stylishly tailored and so long.

She twisted round and looked down her skirt; it was short enough to reveal her feet. And they were large.

Well I know for certain that if I only had the money, I wouldn't wear this ragamuffin outfit another single day, she thought. And she resumed her previous position.

But it would still be annoying, if he were to think he could take liberties. She would not let him do it again. Would it be proper for her to tell him so? ... Oh, she would be so embarrassed

29

at even mentioning something like that! But what should one do then? Look stern. But if he pretended not to understand? Ugh!

Look, there he was. As fat and red as ever.

She sat watching him, running her fingers through her yellow fringe.

The Squire did not look up. Even on the steps he and the Rector continued their conversation in low, urgent tones.

It must be 'business', thought Selma.

As the coach rumbled away, she stood watching it go. Even the sound was so distinguished – a dull ringing which delighted her. And what horses!

But the letter!

She hurried down to her uncle's room. He was standing by the desk with his back to her.

'Have you had a letter from Papa, Uncle?'

He turned and looked at her.

'Yes, I have had a letter,' he said slowly, adjusting his gold-rimmed spectacles on his nose, 'but it is not a letter that will please you.'

'Why? Is something wrong?' she said urgently, going pale.

'No, but Magnus does not want to let you go to Stockholm.'

'Doesn't he?'

'No.'

'Was there no letter to me?'

'No.'

'May I read yours, Uncle?'

'No. Your father has asked me to discuss this with you. Having given the matter further consideration, I believe he is right.'

'Right about what?'

'You are still too young to be thinking of such things.'

'Too young, too young? I'm getting older with every passing day, you know.'

'Indeed so. That is why you must wait a few years.'

'No, it won't do; I must start now, so time is on my side. It is a slow process. Later, it will be too late. Later, I won't want to.'

He picked up a pen and tested the point against his nail.

'Then you must give up the idea.'

He spoke calmly, in a low voice, as was his wont, but with the certainty that has the power to impress.

Her lip trembled with suppressed emotion.

'But Uncle ... ,' she could hardly get the words out, 'you must help me, Uncle.'

She went over to him and, looking up into his face, put an imploring hand on his arm. It was an imperviously smooth face, never showing any emotion.

'Not this time,' he said, stroking her hair calmly and clerically.

She, too, tried to appear calm.

'It isn't just a passing fancy, Uncle,' she said without looking up. 'You know that I am not as childish as I sometimes seem. Papa has never had anyone but me, after all, and I soon had to learn how to think. We have been such friends, he and I, and if he really understands how much this matters to me, I'm sure he won't say no. But he depends on you so much, Uncle, in business and in other things, and if you set yourself against it, there is nothing I can do. That is why you must help me. You know how hard I've always worked when it comes to drawing. You have often praised me yourself, Uncle, and that has spurred me on. Now I want to do it so much that I can't stop myself. You needn't think I shall tire of it or lose heart, if only I can devote myself to what I want to do – wood-carving or sketching or anything along those lines. But I am no good as a housekeeper. You see, I shall get on and be a credit to you, if I am only allowed to try. Please don't say no.'

'Child, now you are being foolish.'

'No I'm not. I know that everything requires work, and that one can only rely on oneself – that has always been poor Papa's mistake, being too easy-going – and it is only to begin with that I need you; then I shall certainly find some solution.'

'Do I usually let you haggle with me, once I have said no?'

She looked quickly up into his face.

'I can make my way by begging, if I have to.'

She made for the door.

'Selma!' There was a sharp edge to his voice.

She turned.

'Do not try anything silly. Runaway children and madhouse inmates are a matter for the police. Do you not know that?'

He smiled – that smooth, cold smile which was his most lethal weapon and which she had hitherto only seen used against others.

It brought her back to her senses with a jolt, but her face was as white as a sheet.

'I am neither a child nor a madwoman, and you can rest assured that I will never go begging. I know I am tied. I have no option but to resign myself to the inevitable.'

She left the room.

When she had gone, the Rector sat down to write to his brother. Selma made no further attempts. She knew her uncle well enough to realize that it would achieve nothing. A deep depression had descended on her, she was not herself. The uninhibited, boyish ways had gone, and been replaced by a stillness in her manner that made her a different person.

As soon as they had eaten their evening meal, she asked to go to bed; she felt so tired.

The Rector and his wife were left alone.

He lay on the sofa as usual. But she had no knitting, for it was Saturday evening.

'Have you told her yet?' asked Mrs Berg, leafing through a copy of *Family Journal*.

'No, I saw no point in doing it today, after she had had that disappointment about the Stockholm trip. Once she has slept on it, I am sure she will calm down.'

'I do not think there is any need for that, I have not seen her so calm for as long as I can remember. It has been a real relief today.'

He merely gave a sneer, which escaped his wife's notice.

'What do you think Richard will have to say about it?' she went on.

'Who do you expect to take his whims into account? A young student – pah! ... he will have time to fall in love a dozen times before he has enough to marry on.'

'But my dear, what do you think they see in the girl? I would go so far as to say that she is actually ugly.'

'Oh no, she could never be called ugly, and besides, she has that appeal – that freshness, you see. Like a lovely winter fruit.'

'Such notions! But I wonder what she is finding to do up there. She could hardly go to bed this early; I think I must just go and see.'

Mrs Berg went, and it was not long before she returned.

'She is sobbing so dreadfully that I can't get a word out of her, but she is in bed, after all.' Mrs Berg set down the lamp she had been carrying.

'It is quite unchristian to be so upset about something so trivial,' she went on.

There were sorrows which Mrs Berg could understand, but there were also those which lay outside her experience. The former included illnesses and deaths in the family, along with burglars, fires and burning the roast. But a sorrow such as Selma's was utterly incomprehensible to her.

'I think I shall go up and speak to her,' said the Rector doubtfully.

He felt so sorry now. Selma was crying. His quick, clever Selma!

'I shall come with you,' said Mrs Berg firmly, sounding pleased. She was expecting a bit of a sensation.

'No, you stay here, I prefer to do this alone,' replied the Rector. There was an antipathy between Selma and her aunt that made the girl stubborn.

He took the lamp and went up to the little attic bedroom, busied himself at the table for a moment and then looked over to the couch. Selma had turned to the wall and pulled the cover over her head. She apparently wanted him to think that she was asleep. He went over and put his hand on her shoulder. She was shuddering with suppressed sobs, but not a sound could be heard.

He felt moved by the fact that she was trying to control herself.

'Child,' he said, 'you know I want what is best for you.'

That was too much. His kindliness only made it more difficult, and he heard a half-stifled sob.

'Have a good cry,' he said. 'It will be a relief for you.'

She must have stuffed the cover in her mouth, for she was suddenly still and quiet.

'It feels hard to bear now,' he said softly. 'It always does, when our illusions are shattered. Do you not think that I, too, have had the same feelings? But the more soberly we can learn to see life, the better it is for us.'

'That's what I'm trying to do,' came the curt, flat reply.

'I know you are. I know you want to be sensible. But you still have a lot to learn. And believe me, the person who can say with a humble heart: "Lord, Thy will be done," is the one who will go most easily through this world. Remember that He is in charge and that you are in His hands.'

'That doesn't make me any less unhappy.'

'Those are ungodly words.'

'What I mean is, that he is in charge of us all,' said a voice from under the cover. 'He is in charge of the unhappiest too, even those who know nothing but sorrow and wretchedness. So *that* is no comfort.'

'Child, what a thing to say!' he said severely.

'Well after all, it won't stop me feeling worse about it, the longer I live. Why not me, along with all the rest?'

'We must seek refuge with Him through prayer.'

This mild pronouncement conflicted so oddly with his whole person, with the formal, elegant posture, with the smooth, indifferent face and with his self-satisfied smile as he uttered them.

'I *have* prayed,' came the rather sullen reply.

'But you have done so in a short-sighted and impatient way. Perhaps there is a happiness awaiting you, such as you never dreamt of.'

'Oh yes, very likely!' sobbed the unbelieving voice under the cover.

He could not hold back a smile, possessing as he did a certain sense of humour; it was the mitigating feature of his character.

The little altercation seemed to have done her good, even

though the grounds for his consolation left her unmoved. The sobs only came intermittently, like a storm subsiding.

'As a consolation, I thought I would give you a little surprise,' he said with a sly smile. 'Do you want to know what it is?'

A protracted sob was her only answer.

'But look here, you are usually so pleased with money.'

He expected to see a pair of swollen eyes peeping out, but the cover remained in place.

'I don't need any money *now*.'

'But a hundred kronor note.'

He had not reached the end of the sentence before she sat up in bed, blinking her red-rimmed eyes in the light.

There really was a banknote lying on the cover.

'Well, what do I want it for now?' she burst out, leaning her forehead against the wall.

'You must work that out for yourself, naturally.'

'Am I to do what I like with it?'

'Of course.'

She did not turn round, but it was clear that the fortress was about to capitulate.

'And I needn't account for how I spend it?'

'No.'

Smiling, he watched the white, nightgowned back and a yellow plait, which hung down over it like a lion's tail. Perhaps she suspected a trap. He almost liked her for that.

'If you threw it down in the road, I should not concern myself,' he went on. 'I only wanted to show you that I do not want to be mean and hard.'

A certain natural weakness had come into his voice.

'Does Aunt know about it?'

She turned, cocked her head on one side and looked over her shoulder.

'No.'

He could scarcely stop himself from laughing. She was as cautious as a village pump lawyer.

'I see,' she said, turning to sit properly on the couch. 'Well, I certainly would like the money, but I can't cheer up all at once because of *that*, so if that's what you hoped, Uncle ...'

Now he really did laugh.

She looked at him most seriously, rather offended.

'You need only say: "Thank you, Uncle,"' he said. 'That is all I ask.'

'Yes, Uncle, I do thank you, but it is an awful lot of money.' She held out her hand limply, and the deal was done.

'I expect you will have to manage more than that in your lifetime; you seem to be quite acquisitive.'

'Yes, I'm sure you're right,' she said with conviction. 'Because without it, nothing can come of anything, as I've so often told Papa. But he has got himself so completely into a corner, he can never get out again.'

'Good night then, my child,' said the Rector, taking her head in his hands and kissing her. Then he turned to go.

She was suddenly gripped by a superstitious horror. She looked at the banknote; the largest sum she had ever owned. Wasn't it blood money? What had she sold? Something within herself ... her own suffering – and for money! ... She thought of Judas.

'Uncle!' she called, just as he reached for the lamp. There was something almost agonized in her voice.

As he turned, she stretched both arms out towards him, as if seeking protection, or begging forgiveness for something.

He went over to her and sat on the edge of the couch.

'Be fond of me. Just a little, little bit. Oh – I'm so unhappy!' She threw her arms around his neck.

He sat there for a moment and let her bury her tear-stained face in the material of his cassock. But he felt no regret, nor did he take back the banknote. He had acted generously and magnanimously, after all, and his conscience was clear.

'Is it a sin, is it a sin?' she cried passionately.

'What? Is what a sin?'

'The money, the money! – Taking payment.'

'How can you talk like that? I give it to you gladly.'

'No, it is *not* a sin,' she said with a deep breath, convulsive as a sob.

36

Chapter 3

When Selma awoke the next morning, she felt heavy and listless. Her aunt came to fetch her for church, but she was not ready, and promised to come on behind. She completed her toilette in great haste, and last of all slipped the hundred kronor note inside the cuff of her dress sleeve, where she fastened it with a pin.

The service had already begun as she approached the church, and the organ was playing. She would have liked to sit on a bench and enjoy the beautiful autumn weather, but that would certainly be frowned on. How fresh it all felt here! ... and so peaceful. A heavy dew covered the matted grass, giving it a bluish tinge; the air was cool and felt so soothing to her burning eyelids. She could feel a weight on her chest and her breathing was deep and laboured as she tried to shift it.

She entered the church to find that all the rows of pews nearest the front were full, so she found a place far back below the gallery, behind a pillar. It was a lower pew than the rest, and she was alone there. That was what she wanted. With great difficulty she found the right verse of the hymn, but her hands were shaking, and it was a strain to hold the book. What could it be that was making her so nervous? Was it the music, or the emotion of the day before, or perhaps simply the fact that she had eaten nothing for breakfast? She put down the book and sank lower in her seat, glad that she had found such a secluded place.

How oddly poignant the hymn singing was today! She would have liked to pray, but could not, for she really had no religion. Or if she did, then it resulted in a strange paradox: I don't believe in God, therefore he will punish me.

Today in particular she felt it so vividly, both that she did not believe and that He would punish her.

The Rector climbed up to the pulpit. From where she was sitting she could not see him, and his words made an impression quite different from usual. His voice came into its own, and was possessed of an uncommon power.

Its effect, however, was weakened by his facial expression, which retained its coldness even when emotion seemed to throb in his voice.

It was not a strong voice, and forcing it would have made it shrill. He therefore kept it low and subdued. But he held his listeners' interest in what he was saying by a masterly modulation that lent the sermon both strength and variety, without straining his vocal resources.

The fourth commandment was the subject of his sermon, and he spoke of how damnation and destruction await those who rebel against their fathers and mothers; how the hand of the Lord would lie heavily on their heads, and how earthly happiness would never blossom in their paths. There seemed to be something concealed behind his very tone, some mysteriously crushing judgement, and a shiver ran through her.

How dreadful it would be to drag out one's whole existence under such a curse – to be doomed irrevocably to misfortune!

For as long as she listened to him, she had to believe; she always did. It was only later she began to doubt.

It was so gloomy down there below the gallery, where she sat behind the pillar as though hidden from the rest of the congregation. A strange anxiety came over her, as if death and judgement were at hand and she an evil-doer about to be struck down. For she did indeed have that quarrelsome sort of nature that could rebel against a father and mother, if ... She did not finish, because now his voice was gentler.

He reminded them that there is only one commandment in which the Lord promises that obedience will bring earthly happiness. And he slowly pronounced: 'That thy days may be long in the land which the Lord thy God giveth thee.' It sounded like something quite new; it was no longer the worn old catechism lesson she had learnt in her childhood; it was something great and glorious that made her breathe a sigh of relief.

Then he paused.

And slowly, almost dreamily, came the exegesis. He spoke of how happiness can be so profound that it outweighs a whole lifetime, even if it cannot be counted long in terms of years; he made it clear that it is parental blessing which builds nests for children, and he spread this blessing like the softest of carpets over all the thorns of life.

Selma's spirits plummeted. She felt she had sacrificed everything to obedience, all that she had loved and hoped for. Was he going to demand more ... more ... ? What would she not willingly give for a single one of those glimpses of the sun, sufficient to outweigh a whole lifetime!

When the last hymn had been sung, she had to stay in her place for a moment to give the traces of her emotion time to subside. Meanwhile, the throng had reached her pew, and she was obliged to wait until the crowd had gone.

She leant up against the pillar and watched the country people as they passed. There was Old Mother Möller, with her daughter. The latter was all tasselled and frilled, dressed in an outfit elegant enough for a lady from town, although she was wearing a scarf on her head – a heavy silk scarf with fringes nearly a foot long – and she came strutting down the aisle with an expression that seemed to say: look at me, look at me! Her mother walked beside her, preening herself and pursing her lips, so her nose looked even more pointed than usual. Coming abreast of Selma's pew, she looked in, and her critical eye swept disdainfully over the old summer coat and came to rest on a glove which perhaps did not sit as neatly as it might have done. Selma inclined her head in greeting, but she pretended not to see.

It was a calculated insult, and Selma flushed crimson. 'Old shrew!' she thought in her colourful, boarding-school vocabulary, indignation seething inside her.

The queue gradually shortened, and she went out. Further up the aisle she could see Axel Möller; he would have to come past her. She made her way through the crowd as quickly as she could, and once she was out in the churchyard, where the local people were dispersing, she stopped by a grave and waited for her aunt, who had stopped at the church door to speak to some farmers' wives. Feeling herself tremble, she put her hand on the iron railings of the grave for support. He would have to pass close by her here.

He flushed a little and came straight towards her.

'I shall go along the railway embankment at four o'clock, meet me there; I have something to tell you,' she said quickly, and then turned away, as if they had merely exchanged greetings. At that moment, her aunt approached, and she went towards her.

'Child, how pale you are,' said her aunt, 'Are you ill?'

'My chest feels tight and my head aches.'

'You are usually in such good health!'

'But Aunt, you know I tend to be anaemic,' she answered in a listless tone, but with a mournful smile, unlike her usual one.

They went home in silence.

The atmosphere at the dinner table was rather flat. Selma, who was usually either talking, or enlivening the others with her ideas and antics, was today utterly quiet and still, and it was left almost entirely to the Rector to keep the conversation going. His attentiveness to his niece was also striking; he treated her in every respect as a grown-up lady. Her aunt sat watching it all. It irritated her.

Now they would just see what a splendid wife that slip of a girl might make! For there was no doubting that Squire Kristerson was rich, and would surely grow richer still in time, for in spite of his impassive air he was a very competent farmer, and that country estate he had bought was considered a good investment. She would of course be given everything she so much as pointed at – young wives always are. And naturally she would soon learn to stick her nose in the air – they so easily do – and perhaps she would even be drawn by a team of horses when she came to visit!

Mrs Berg cast a furious sideways look at Selma.

How could people see anything pretty about the girl! She was as ugly as sin. And even her own Richard ... hadn't he been most interested in her? They always seemed to be quarrelling, to be sure, but the truth was that he neither heard nor saw anyone but her. Her maternal pride was thoroughly wounded by his lack of taste. He had talked of her freshness. Stuff and nonsense! My goodness, today she looked as pale and puffy-eyed as if she had sat up for ten nights in a row; oh yes, just give her a few years, and the freshness would be gone soon enough. It made one quite sick. And what large hands! – What was it Berg had said the night before? It was enough to make one feel quite ill. And girls like her were going and getting married! ... without even being able to make proper gravy for the roast. But she wanted no part of the business. She would let Berg do as he pleased, but there was no doubt that he would bring them together in the end.

'You look positively wretched today,' said the Rector to his niece, 'You ought to have a little after-dinner nap.'

'No, I'd rather go out for a walk,' replied Selma, 'I feel as dead as a fly in October, that's all. I must pull myself together.'

'Yes, whatever you feel up to, as long as you don't go around looking so glum. It won't do.'

'Oh, it never lasts for long,' she answered, with an attempt at her usual briskness, 'I shall just spit on my hands and get a better grip.'

'Oh really, Selma!', her aunt burst out reproachfully. She was glad of the excuse.

'Don't worry, Aunt, I can't do it today, but perhaps tomorrow,' answered Selma with a laugh, raising her light grey eyes, their colour dulled by crying, but their mischievous look still intact.

Her uncle gave her a nod of encouragement, much to his wife's chagrin.

As soon as her elders had gone to take their nap, Selma went out.

She chose the path that took her to the gate and through to the railway track. Her step was as brisk as usual, but the carefree expression on her face had given way to a resigned, earnest look. The exercise and fresh air did however give her some colour.

Before she was halfway to the other level crossing, she saw the young man walking towards her. Her heart was beating

41

audibly; it would be hard to find the words, but her mind was made up.

As they came up to each other, she gave a cursory nod and turned about, so that they were then walking side by side in the direction of the rectory. They walked together for a while. She was hunting for some opening words and he was feeling uncomfortable. This was a formal meeting arranged by her, and that was not quite proper for a girl, he felt. It had made her sink in his estimation; he viewed her more soberly and no longer felt her so superior.

'I overestimated myself,' she began in a subdued voice, betraying some emotion. ' I can't persuade Uncle to let me go, and I must stay here.'

She was silent for a moment. Her chest felt so tight, she coughed a little to clear her voice.

'It is quite different for us women than for you men,' she said with an earnestness that sounded incongruously old and wise. 'For you, it is considered a duty to strive for independence; for us, that is almost a fault, unless we are old maids. I thought before that everything was a matter of money, but it isn't. Even if I had money, I would still not get away now. I did think for a while of trying anyway, that is, of going without permission and asking someone else to help, but it wouldn't work; I see that now. People would just think I was mad and laugh at me. And besides ... I don't know what came over me in church today ... it seems to me that if I did, I would be dogged by misfortune! That is something I could never bear. So it's better not to try.'

He walked in silence, listening. Was *this* what she wanted to say! – It was still a strange idea to arrange to meet him.

'For you, it's a different matter,' she went on eagerly, 'None of that applies in your case. You shall have my money – I have a hundred kronor with me, which are quite my own – and you shall go away and find employment, any sort you like, as long as you get on.'

'That's impossible,' he replied, on the verge of alarm. In the face of this startling energy he felt as if he were standing by a stretch of water and could expect to be pushed into it at any moment.

'Impossible?' she repeated, and gave a snort. 'What is the matter now! Before it was just money, or so you said.'

'But mother doesn't want me to. What you said about bad luck would surely apply to me too.'

'Have you ever heard of a man whose luck ran out because he went his own way? No, if anyone is to have bad luck, it will be me, you may be sure; I can feel it.'

'But since you yourself cannot, why ... ?'

'For that very reason. It's precisely because I can't myself be what I want, that I can't bear to see you staying on here and making nothing of your life either. Don't you understand?'

'And if I were to accept your ... ?'

'Yes, what of it? You don't think I care about money now? I could just as well throw it down in the street, for that matter. You needn't have any scruples about it. You know yourself that you are on the wrong track; find a new profession right away.'

'But how far do you think one can get with ... '

She gave a start, and a burning blush spread over her face and right down to her neck. The sum was too small. All at once she realized. She had not thought of it before; it had seemed such a lot to her. And now she felt the shame of having made herself ridiculous.

'Uncle is quite right to say that I'm a child. But I shall not stay one for long,' she thought. She was filled with such indignation and shame that she wished the earth would swallow her up. She neither said a word nor looked at him, but began to walk more briskly. He matched her pace, but could think of nothing to say. It was equally awkward for both of them. He was sure of only one thing, and that was that he had distressed her. He felt an acute need to make amends.

'I am sure you can imagine how grateful ...'

'Please just stop talking about it,' she burst out, 'It was so stupid, so utterly stupid. As if *that* was worth offering you! But that's just like me.'

'And to think that for my sake, you ... '

'Be quiet!' she cried, the colour draining from her face. 'It

43

makes me angry just to hear it, and if you breathe a word to anyone...'

Her pupils dilated until her eyes were almost black, and she came to a halt in front of him.

'For goodness' sake ... I only meant ... ,' he said apologetically, his stooped, narrow-shouldered figure seeming to shrink still further.

'All right, so keep quiet about it,' she said roughly, and they walked on.

'For you, or for anyone else in your position,' she resumed after a while, 'it would have been all the same. I told you that's what I was like.'

They had reached the crossing by the rectory.

'This is where we part,' she said.

He stayed silent. It all oppressed him so.

Selma stepped up on to one of the large boulders by the wayside, put her hand on the gatepost and looked out over the countryside. The fields lay reaped and deserted. Not a single human being for as far as the eye could see, but in the distance the blue, hazy outlines of forest and mountain ridge were visible, and below them glinted an inlet of the lake. She took it all in with a long look. It seemed like a farewell.

'And yet, it is lovely here,' she said with a sigh, 'I would have liked to be an artist.'

As she lowered her gaze, she caught sight of a little wagtail, running about in a field of stubble, her tail constantly bobbing as she lifted it high, so it would be out of her way. And then off she ran, as fast as her little legs would carry her!

Selma was enchanted. She had forgotten Mr Möller and all the world. Her gaze followed the actions of the bird, she was smiling broadly, revealing all her teeth, and her eyes were bright. There she stood, so full of sparkle and life herself, illuminated by the setting sun.

And down below, the wagtail darted about with her neat little movements. Now and then she paused, gave a little nod, located something else to snatch up, and was off in a new direction.

Finally Selma looked down at her companion. He looked

embarrassed and was poking amongst the stones with his stick.

'Goodbye,' she said quickly, as she jumped down. 'Good luck.'

He had been lost in thought and gave a start at her tone. There was a bitter, taunting element in it. The gate slammed shut and she went on down the road with her usual, wilful step and her hands in her coat pockets.

He remained at the roadside, following her with his eyes; she turned in at the garden gate of the rectory, and vanished from his sight.

The very sunlight seemed to darken with the feeling of disappointment that crept over him, along with some self-reproach. How he had interpreted her ... how he had behaved ... and how many things he should not have said! How significant these minutes could have been, if he had known how to use them! He could have confessed all his thoughts and feelings to her! She would have understood him.

Now the opportunity was gone and might perhaps never return.

Her cheerful disposition had a mysterious power over him, and he was never as keenly aware of it as each time they parted. It felt as though she were taking with her something of his inner self, which had to be painfully torn loose, and today it was worse than ever.

He threw himself down on the mound of stones under the trees. It was as if the whole world were dead and he alone still living, with his feelings of regret and loss. For she would never come again, he sensed it, and his only comfort was to inflict further hurt upon himself by conjuring up in his mind all that might have been and was not. He positively enjoyed torturing himself with all the possibilities, and buried himself in bottomless emptiness, driven by the desire to experience it to its fullest extent.

'Never, never!' he repeated, and each time he felt as if his heart would break. Couldn't one die of that... simply die?

In his diseased imagination, she appeared all at once as something infinitely remote and divinely beautiful.

Morose and downcast, Selma reached home. She too felt emptiness, but of a different kind. Until now, she had spent every spare moment constructing plans for the future and castles in the air. Now they were all thrown over, and she was left regarding the wreckage and not knowing what to do. What could fill up her life now, what was there to hope for, to strive for? And behind it all, the shame burned on – the shame of having given herself away, of having made a fool of herself, of having been rejected.

She went to her special place in the dining room window, where she would often sit looking down on the chickens and doves. That was her way of passing the time, when she was in low spirits.

Her uncle and aunt came in, fresh from their nap, and they took coffee in silence. Then Selma resumed her place, and Mrs Berg left the room. Her husband remained, and went over to the other window.

'Kristerson will be coming over this evening,' he said. 'You ought to give him a game, it would cheer you up.'

'Oh, should I! We always quarrel; that's what happened last time.'

She craned her neck in order to see a blue, male dove, bobbing its head and going round in circles down in the courtyard, complaining excitedly.

'Indeed, but I do believe there would be no pleasure in it for either of you, without all the bickering,' remarked the Rector with a smile.

'That may be, but the Squire isn't anywhere near as annoying as Richard. Won't he be home before St. Martin's Eve?'

'No. Are you missing him?'

'Oh – no. But I thought he would come home for your birthday, Uncle.'

She pulled a disapproving face, and silence fell for a moment.

'Tell me honestly what you think of Kristerson,' the Rector asked after a while.

She took her time before she answered, putting her head out of the window to get a better view. The short-legged cockerel had picked a fight with the long-legged one. Who would be the victor?

She drew her head in again.

'Well, he's nice enough, but he's dreadfully fat.'

'An uncommonly fine fellow.'

She looked out into the courtyard again, fascinated by the cockfight. Her uncle watched too, but without interest.

'Oh Uncle! I never thought that the little one would have such spirit,' Selma burst out in admiration.

'Why not? Small men ...'

She gave a laugh.

'Yes, but small cockerels!'

'You can be remarkably childish sometimes.' There was a touch of impatience in the Rector's tone.

She turned right round and sat down on the chair, so she was looking him straight in the eye.

'Yes, so I can, but I shall put all that behind me now. If only I could fathom what in the world I am going to be.'

She could not resist the temptation to cast a sideways look out into the courtyard, and saw to her annoyance that the larger cockerel definitely had the advantage.

'I believe I can give you some good advice in that respect,' said her uncle.

'Can't you separate them? They're scratching each other's eyes out,' she called in agitation to one of the maids, who was crossing the courtyard.

'*Child*! May we not leave the cockerels to their own devices for the moment? There is something I really must speak to you about,' said her uncle impatiently. 'Come down to my room.'

'There's no need. Coming away from the window will be enough for me.' She went over and sat on the dining table. 'What is it, then?'

He would have preferred her to adopt a more appropriate position than sitting there swinging her legs, but he decided it was not worth fussing over details now.

'I wanted to talk about you future. I do not think you could do any better than becoming the wife of a good fellow.'

'Yes, but if had to wait about for *that*, then ...'

47

'But you do not need to wait about. Kristerson has requested me to ask you if you will become his wife.'

She stopped swinging her legs to and fro, and looked up, with an expression of careless enquiry.

'Er, no,' she said, and went back to her swinging. There was a brief pause. Then she jumped down from the table and went over to the window.

'Was that all you wanted to say, Uncle?' she asked, turning to face him.

'All? – The most important step in life.'

'Well yes, of course,' she readily admitted. 'If one actually *gets* married.'

'One should certainly at the very least give the possibility some consideration, if one wishes to be seen as a sensible person.'

She sank down onto the chair in near desperation, and clasped her hands in her lap.

'If only I could see what he wanted me for!'

The Rector turned and looked out of the window. A smile touched his lips.

'He likes you, of course.'

'And you think I should take him, Uncle?'

'You should at least give it some consideration.'

She began to look thoughtful. The hens let out a collective shriek, but she did not deign even to glance at them.

'What would be the good of it? I wouldn't know how to keep house!'

'Nor would you need to. I do not think Kristerson would even contemplate it.'

She grew more thoughtful still.

'I wonder what Papa would think.'

'For him, it would naturally be a source of enormous joy. He has worries enough on his own account and Kristerson is the sort of fellow anyone would be glad to have for a son-in-law.'

'So you think that Papa would *want* me to?'

'Indeed I do.'

She was silent for a moment.

'But to marry him! ... You know, Uncle, it's a question of respect.'

'What do you mean?'

'Oh – he's so fat, and he looks like a shaven pig.'

'But child!'

'Yes, and he's the same age as Papa, too.'

'What of it? Magnus is young enough to go off and find you a stepmother any day, and think how pleasant it would be for you at home then. Much better to have a place of your own.'

'Huh! Papa certainly couldn't afford to get married,' she exclaimed with a laugh. 'So you're only trying to frighten me.'

The Rector said nothing. One had to tread so warily; she really was more cunning than one might give her credit for. He drummed on the window frame and assumed an air of indifference. It seemed as though he intended to let the subject drop.

This time, she was the one who took it up again.

'And I'm so young, I might find that I liked someone else, after all,' she said.

'Liked? ... after you were married! ... surely there could never be any question of that,' he said slowly and disapprovingly. Then he turned round to face her abruptly, as if a new thought had just struck him.

'But of course. I have seen you and young Möller out walking together on several occasions – does that have any bearing on the matter? You haven't gone and taken a fancy to him?'

She blushed furiously.

'I! Fancy ... ? No, not at all.'

'Ah, it only occurred to me because you would not listen to the other idea. But in any case, let me tell you that it is not worth building your hopes on, because he will eventually be paired off with Jöns Ols' Marie, you may be sure. You must realize that the Möllers are the sort of people who look for money.'

'Oh! He may marry whom he chooses, so I might as well have the Squire, for that matter.'

She meant what she said, and yet was seething with indignation, wondering whether he had been thinking of Jöns Ols' Marie when he rejected her paltry hundred kronor.

Her blush deepened, to her extreme mortification, but the Rector pretended not to see.

'This autumn, Kristerson is planning to move to that country estate he has bought; they say it is very beautiful there,' he said.

'He has got terribly elegant horses,' she remarked.

The Rector said nothing. It was starting to work, and now he wanted to give her time.

'When one is as rich as he is, one can have whatever one wants,' he observed after a while.

'Is he really that rich?'

'That I can guarantee,' replied the Rector.

There was silence. She was thinking of a tall, grey horse ... or perhaps one that was completely black. And a riding habit with a train, to be carried over the arm ... a ladies' saddle of the new light and compact design ... and naturally a servant lad at the stirrup: when one is that rich, one can have whatever one wants.

She looked down and very carefully pleated the trimming on her dress.

'Do you think he would keep a horse for me to ride, Uncle?'

The question came very timidly. A single word could frighten her off. One had to bargain with this child as carefully as with the Devil himself over the soul of a sinner.

'Well, on an estate like that, the stables are full of horses,' the Rector said carelessly.

He knew these waters, and however pluckily the little craft resisted the wind at first, it would take only one more gust to throw her off course. He was sure of it.

'I'm so young,' she said. It was her last, feeble protest.

'Yes. It is a rare honour to get an offer like this at your tender age, and I really do not know what you have done to deserve it,' he answered with his best smile.

This appealed to her vanity. Engaged so young ... it would cause quite a stir!

The pallor of her face was relieved only by two vivid red patches, extending from her cheeks down to her neck, and disfiguring the young face with their signs of agitation and passion. She looked at her left hand. It would be nice to see how it looked with the engagement ring! ... a thick, weighty ring of twenty carat gold.

What would Old Mother Möller do now? She saw in her mind's eye the mocking look that had swept over the outgrown coat. Her eyes flashed and she looked up.

'I look pretty poor,' she said, showing the insides of her dress sleeves to prove how worn they were. 'It would be too awkward if *he* had to buy me new clothes.'

'I shall provide everything you need; I am only too happy to do it for my only niece.'

He was so delighted with his victory. He opened his arms to her with an unaccustomed cordiality.

She came skipping over to him, threw her arms around his neck and looked at him out of two pale-grey eyes, sparkling with appetite for life. Her thick, wavy hair fell low over her forehead, and her startling red lips smiled at the thought of all the envy she would arouse.

All at once, she was serious.

'Uncle dear, do you think he is going to like me?' she said. She had a habit of using that 'dear' as a term of endearment.

'I am sure of it.'

A sunny smile flashed across her face and a new thought through her innocent mind. Now she was almost beautiful.

... If he were to like her enough ... !

All her old plans and castles in the air rose up again.

The Rector stroked her hair: he had nothing more to say.

Chapter 4

Squire Kristerson's father had been a veterinary surgeon, and his practice had enabled him to save a modest capital for his son. The son was not one for books, and so became a farmer. He was doggedly persistent and had quite a shrewd head for business, as well as being bold and rather lucky besides.

The father had to be very careful with his money in order to scrape together the capital. This meant that the son became familiar with the pressures of straitened circumstances and learnt to appreciate money, because he had to do without it. The old man's admonitions therefore fell on fertile ground, and grew into one particular ambition: money. That was the key to everything else.

The Squire had spent the years of his youth in restless activity. Horse trading, aquavit, and oxen for the slaughterhouse had enabled him to come up in the world, but he had long since finished with the horse dealing and the distillery business, as his working capital was now more than enough, and he was a competent farmer.

He had often thought of marriage, but had made up his mind that a hundred thousand kronor was the minimum his chosen one should bring with her, and as he was no beauty, with his shiny red face and little piggy eyes, the heiresses had all passed him by. But this had never caused him any heartache. Things were fine as they were. At the time when he had needed to work hardest, he had managed on his own, and now – now he could enjoy the good times – he felt the lack of a wife even less. As far as the hundred thousand were concerned, he no longer cared about them.

He had never had any real schooling, for since he had not wanted to study, his father had considered it unnecessary to waste money on any kind of tuition. But he had read quite a few novels and serialized fiction, and kept up with the events of the day in his newspaper, which had given him a reputation as one of the best-educated farmers in the neighbourhood. With his male friends he could be coarse, but in the company of ladies he was courtesy personified, and in his reading, he was insistent on 'a poetic interpretation of life', that is, lots of love and feminine 'sweetness' (he was very attached to the word), swooning young misses in white dresses, vile villains, a murder or two to make the whole thing more 'exciting', plus – naturally – a few weddings at the end, for virtue must have its reward, after all, at least if it was a story with any kind of moral purpose.

He liked English novels best, and most of all those written by ladies. He detested the immorality of French novels. He liked to mention the fact in the company of ladies; it made such a good impression.

Sometimes, lying reading on his sofa, he would find a book so moving that he had to dab at his eyes. He would tell people about it afterwards, as proof of his warm heart; and with a sly glance out of the corner of his eye, he would observe how attentively certain ladies were listening, almost as if infected by his emotion. Oh yes, money is power! But there was no hurry.

And then he met Selma.

It had been towards the end of the previous winter. He and the Rector were sitting in the rectory parlour, chatting over a glass of arrack punch. The lamps had just been lit. But no one had said a word about there being a young girl in the house and he was taken by surprise when she opened the door and came in, flushed and warm, with a pair of skates thrown carelessly over her arm and clattering with every step she took. Her hair was matted with the warmth, the bodice of her dress disordered by the vigorous exercise, and she was blinking in the light. She came into the lamplight and gave him her hand with a pert curtsey, as the Rector introduced her, and jokingly added that she had come to them to learn a few manners, which would certainly not come amiss.

She merely laughed, and did not seem at all disconcerted by the Squire being so slow to release her hand, where her pulse was racing with warmth and vitality.

'That was quick, that was quick,' he said, and scarcely knew what he was saying.

But he smiled and she smiled, and it was as if his head was swimming and he was young again. Her clothes had brought the cold winter air in with them, and her lips shone red and warm. He did not know what came over him; he could have leapt to his feet and taken her in his arms for sheer delight in her spirit and youth.

Then he let go of her hand and gave her an appraising look.

She was tall in stature, with broad shoulders, long arms and large hands. Her figure was not fully-grown; there was something half-finished and odd about the whole strong, angular form. But no matter – no matter – child or not: she must be his!

This was what the Squire was thinking as his comfortable carriage bore him along the road on his way to propose.

But he had definitely not been of one mind throughout. He had sobered up at intervals and considered the whole idea a whim, a flight of fancy. And then he would pay a call at the rectory to convince himself in person that she was – as everyone said – a very plain girl. But each time he saw her, the same thing happened. He could see that she might be called plain, but he simply could not keep his eyes off her. There was not a movement of that body, not a tone of that voice, which did not enchant him, be it called plain or beautiful. What did it matter what other people said! There was something about that fresh, plain look, that held him in a stronger grip than all the beauty in the world. It was nothing generally applicable, nothing he could put his finger on; it was just that she was so very much *herself*.

He could not imagine that she would refuse him, for he was so much in love that it seemed to him she had been meant for him from the beginning, but he had simply not realized it until now.

Looking back over his past, it appeared to him that God had

led him on through a myriad mazes, to this one goal; and that all he called poetry, all he had kept suppressed while the 'hundred thousand' counted for everything and personal feelings for nothing, it all came flooding forth in one great torrent, no longer with its original effervescent freshness, but bubbling with dammed-up sludge. Yet he was glad, even so. It felt as though he himself were young again, because it was a youthful passion that broke down all defences. And this illusion made him happy.

There had never been any room for doubt of *her* happiness: after all, he wanted to give her everything.

As the carriage drove up to the front of the rectory, he awoke as if from a dream. It was growing dark, and lights shone from several windows. He wondered whether she might come out to meet him in person. No, it was the Rector standing there on the steps to welcome him.

Once the guest had hung up his overcoat and hat in the hall, his host invited him into his private rooms. It was warm there, and the lamp was lit.

The Squire felt a little embarrassed. He rubbed his hands with a singular cracking sound, and paced up and down the strip of carpet as if to warm his feet. The Rector checked the lamp and took a moment turning down the flame. It appeared as if they both wanted to win a little time before their conversation began.

Squire Kristerson was tall and heavy-set. The splendid solidity of his bearing gave an impression of strength, but signs of good living had blurred any characteristic facial features to such an extent that they gave no impression of anything, except possibly a replete, self-satisfied confidence. His whole manner seemed to say: I have done *my* bit, and now I am enjoying the fruits of my labours.

The Rector was still standing by his desk. The thin, sihouetted form completely hid the lamp, but the light streamed out on all sides, as if emanating from the dark body itself.

'Well?' said the Squire.

The Rector turned and leant on the desk.

'Yes, all will be well, but first there is one subject I must raise with you.' He pushed his spectacles a little more firmly onto the bridge of his nose, as he always did when he had to speak on a matter of some importance.

The Squire stopped pacing for a moment, and waited.

'It is the matter of your housekeeper.' The Rector broke off and gave a discreet cough.

'Naturally I shall arrange that. She is to move out on the twenty-fourth – I am setting her up with a bakery.'

'Not near here?' The Rector did not raise his head, but a quick, searching look darted from behind the spectacles.

'Goodness me, no – down near Trelleborg, I'm not quite sure where.' The Squire chopped the air with his hand to indicate that he wished her as far away as possible.

'And no promises of marriage, or anything like that?'

'Not a hint – wouldn't dream of it.'

'No, quite right,' said the Rector with satisfaction, raising one hand and contemplating his nails.

There was then a pause, during which the Squire continued pacing to and fro. The Rector's ability to subdue the behaviour of others by his own wary approach meant that people seldom tried to rush any conversation with him if he was taking his time.

'There is one other matter,' he said, his voice feeling its way carefully forward, selecting a word here, another word there. 'I just want to warn you. Well, that is ... do not get me wrong ... but Selma really is an unusual girl, and has to be treated in a very special way. You, with your bachelor habits ... yes yes, I know you're a ladies' man, but not all women are the same, and a girl like Selma has ideas of her own. If you were to offend her in any way – er, quite by accident I mean, of course – it might well be that she would simply send you packing! And once she had done it, no power on earth would make her change her mind.'

'Yes, but what in the world ... !' The Squire came to an abrupt halt in the middle of the room, looking more than ready for a fight.

'Yes, yes, I know!' said the Rector, simultaneously impatient and soothing, and bringing his hand down forcefully with each exclamation. 'But since that's how it *is*, you have no choice but either to accept it or to give up the whole idea now. Until the banns have been read, and so on, no-one can force her. Now I am well aware what a good match it would be for her, and that is precisely why I do not wish to see it thrown over.'

'Do you mean that ... ?' The Squire looked about him, quite at a loss as to how to formulate his question.

'I just mean that a girl like Selma is quite unlike the women you have ... er ... encountered. In a childlike mind such as hers, there is something so timid – something, what shall I say? – something so sensitive. She can take offence at the least thing, at things you would never believe. She must have time to come round, and you must handle her ... well, you must handle her, as if she were a bird you were trying to capture.'

The last words came out rapidly, quite unlike all the rest, and made the Rector give a laugh, short and hollow. Looking at the fat Squire, he found the comparison excessively comical.

'But surely I may be permitted to kiss her, for God's sake!' cried the husband-to-be in an eruption of despair and consternation.

'Ye-es. But if you take my advice, you should not be in too much of a hurry.' The Rector suppressed his urge to smile, but inwardly he was shaking with laughter, and the wide, tight-lipped mouth seemed even wider with that ironic look at the corners.

They fell silent again, and the Squire resumed his pacing.

What a host of preliminaries! And there he had been, dreaming that his love would be like a triumphal march! The state of blissful jubilation into which he had worked himself up slowly subsided, like a dying flame.

'There is naturally no need to postpone the wedding for long,' he said. 'After all, there is nothing to wait for.'

'Nothing more than the banns and the bridal gown,' replied the Rector, now serious. He drew himself up to his full height and invited his guest to come upstairs to join the family.

It cannot be denied that the Squire's heart began beating faster; the whole procedure had a distinct solemnity to it.

The drawing room was brightly lit, but empty.

'Take a seat for a moment; I will call Selma,' said the Rector.

The Squire went over to one of the tables and flung himself down onto a chair. It was so quiet in the room and everything was so extraordinary; the whole house seemed as expectant as he was himself.

Then a door slammed up above, and there were footsteps on the stairs! He could hear them approaching, the door was opened, and Selma came in alone. The Rector went back to his study.

The Squire went forward to meet her and took her hand; it was cold, and trembling slightly. She did not look herself. Her old outspokenness had been replaced by an uncertainty which made even the Squire feel awkward.

'Selma,' was all he said. He sounded almost apologetic, for the paleness of the childlike face seemed to reproach him. But he wanted to make her happy! That was what he wanted.

As she looked up into his face, there was a trace of guilt in her usually uninhibited gaze, but she advanced to the table with her hand in his, and they sat down facing one another. He saw that she had taken trouble over her appearance. Her hair was newly tidied, and she had on her best dress – dark blue with a satin trim.

'I have something to say first,' she began in her deep alto voice, which vibrated a little. 'I have a lot to say. And then you can decide for yourself.'

Two bright red roses came into bloom on her cheeks as she spoke. There was a lamp on the table and the matt white shade directed the light downwards onto her face, making its contrasting hues more evident than ever – that creamy whiteness against the fresh crimson of her lips.

He felt such an urge to kiss her right away, but then he remembered the Rector's warning.

'If I said that what I felt for you was love, I would be lying,' she said, in the tone of a schoolboy reciting part of an epic poem that has become particularly popular. She had clearly prepared her speech. 'But if you really like me – and I think you do – then I am sure I could be fond of you, not as fond as of my Papa, of course, but perhaps as fond as I am, say, of Uncle or my cousin Richard.'

The Squire sat up abruptly.

'Ah, so you are fond of him?'

'Of course. He's the only cousin I have!' She regarded him, almost offended, and at that moment was quite her old self.

'It's not a particularly tempting prospect, being liked as a cousin, but ... '

'It will come, it will come,' he assured her.

'No,' she answered emphatically, 'That's just what I wanted to say, I don't think it ever will.'

He smiled, conscious of knowing infinitely more than she did.

'Oh yes it will,' he said, ' When we are married, it will come.'

'Oh, I don't think it can make that much difference,' she said in a superior tone. 'After all, everyone knows that the engagement is the happiest time.'

He was rendered speechless by all this wisdom. She spoke with as much assurance as if she had been engaged at least a dozen times.

'It isn't that you have taken a liking to someone else?' he asked cautiously.

'No, of course not, I've never been the passionate type.' She considered herself to have an immense period of time over which to look back.

'Well in that case, then ... '

'Yes, that's what I thought, too,' she chimed in brightly, believing she had understood his view. 'And it may be just as well. People are so terribly different, that's all. Some are always going and falling in *love* - ' she drew the word out into a bleating. 'But then there are others who can only be fond of people. And there's a frightfully big difference between those two things, let me tell you.' She paused and looked at him inquiringly to ascertain whether he was following the deeper points of her argument.

He was still sitting thinking of that kiss, which he could not get out of his mind, and so he just nodded. She took it as an acknowledgement.

'Yes, just so,' she said with relief. 'I can't see that there's anything very wonderful about it. There are no more tiresome creatures to see than people in love, and I have often resolved to disprove the notion that I was bound to turn out as sickly-sweet as other engaged girls.'

'You see,' she added more confidentially, 'I hadn't really intended ever to get married. I always thought I would get along quite well on my own. But there seem to be so many *ifs* and *buts* that ... If only I had someone willing to help me a tiny bit! Because I really would still like to make something of myself.'

She stole a furtive glance at him, to see to what extent he might be inclined to fall into this trap.

He was sitting watching her with a drowsy expression in his eyes, rather like the look of someone who is toasting himself in front of the stove and has grown too lazy to move. At least, that was how she thought he looked: face red and shiny, eyelids half-closed.

She coughed rather sharply, and tears of vexation welled up in her eyes.

'I would much rather be something than get married!' she cried, frightened by his fixed smile.

'What do you want to be?' he asked, dragging himself forcibly up out of his lovestruck intoxication.

'A painter,' she said softly. 'Help me do it.' She leant forward, taking his hands and looking up into his face. That lively character could make itself endearing when she wanted it to!

He looked down into those imploring eyes, as clear and many-coloured as the waters of the sea when the wind has dropped and the sun is shining. How beautiful she was!

'You shall do it all, everything you want, if only we can be married,' he said huskily.

'Everything?' She gave him a hesitant, doubtful look.

'Everything, everything! I will never be able to refuse you anything.'

He took her head in his hands and kissed her, just once, quickly and wildly.

The blood rushed to her face and she got up, took out her handkerchief and rubbed at her lips.

'I see,' she said indignantly. '*I see.*' That was all she could get

60

out.

He jumped up and stopped her, just as she was about to open the door to leave.

'I won't do it again,' he cried, 'No, I damned well won't!'

It sounded so genuine that she turned. But she looked at him as if at a strange animal one might suspect of having dangerous intentions.

'Now come and sit down and pretend it never happened.'

'All ri-ight then!' The bittersweet words came out slowly, and she pulled another face.

'Now now, I won't do it again. Once we are married, you will see that ... '

'Indeed I will not!' she interrupted petulantly.

'Let us not argue about it now. Come here.'

He looked wide awake, she thought, and they resumed their seats.

'What were you saying? You mentioned painting, didn't you?'

'Yes.'

She looked sulkily down into her lap and stuck out her lower lip, the way she always did when she was dissatisfied with something.

Some effort was now required on his part, if he wished to restore good relations between them.

'You will have plenty of time to paint after you are married, you shall do whatever you want to.'

She did not reply, merely sat smoothing her dress.

'Now now, it is nothing to get so heated about!' he said playfully, taking her hands in one of his and shaking them, as if to revive her.

She laughed.

'But it was so frightfully stupid of you, Paul ... jumping on someone like that and kissing them, just when they were sitting talking!'

That 'Paul' came so spontaneously that it was music to his ears. He would triumph, he must triumph, at any cost!

'Well, was there anything else you wanted to say?' he asked, with the good humour that was his most appealing characteristic.

'Oh, lots!' she answered, and gave a smile with a hint of self-mockery. 'You can't imagine all the things I'm thinking about, Paul.'

'Let me hear them.'

There was an equality in their relationship now, which they both found delightful. All because of that 'Paul'. She found it so 'comical' to use it to the richest magnate in the neighbourhood, while for him it was like a caress as it stole half shyly, half mischievously from her lips.

Perhaps she was thinking that she had been rather silly and was now trying to make amends. After all, one kiss wasn't the end of the world, although it certainly hadn't been pleasant! But of course, it was all part of being 'engaged'.

'No, let's be serious now,' she said, nudging his elbow, for he seemed all too inclined to treat matters lightheartedly: she could see he was beaming.

'Yes, let's,' he said.

'For a start, there's the fact that you don't know me at all, Paul.'

'I know you enough to like you.'

'I can well believe it! One often likes people, because one knows them too little.' She had an inexhaustible fund of wisdom.

'Well, I can get to know you soon enough,' he said drily.

'Pah! No Paul, I shall tell you exactly what I'm like, so you don't buy a pig in a poke. Will you listen to me?'

'Yes, all right.'

She settled herself in her seat, and as she spoke she nodded her head and counted on her fingers, one by one, with great emphasis.

'Firstly, I detest cooking, and that is a great failing.'

'I can pay a housekeeper; you need not do any cooking.'

'And then I'm quick-tempered.'

'You will calm down, given time.'

'But then I'm a madcap, and I'm obstinate too, and I'm untidy and I'm cheeky, and I offend people by trampling all over their feelings. And if you don't believe me, just ask Aunt.'

He chuckled and looked at her. She was very eager, and was

still holding on tightly to the last finger she had used in her list, while she considered whether there was anything else to declare.

'And I can never, ever fall in love with you.'

That was the end, and she spread out her fingers to show him everything had been said.

'Well, we shall see,' he mumbled.

'No, please be sensible! I tell you I can't. Will you have me anyway?'

'But all the same,' he mumbled.

'Well, you will have only yourself to blame. Don't come along later and say that I tricked you!' She fixed him with a threatening look, as if he were an incorrigible child requiring constant admonitions to behave.

'No, no. But let's be married soon.'

'Well, you must talk to Uncle about that.'

'And now you are my fiancée.' He held out his hand, and she gave him hers solemnly and earnestly.

They sat for a while without speaking; there was so much to think about. She broke the silence.

'You know, I believe it is a good thing that you are so much older than me – now I come to think about it. If you were the same age as me, you wouldn't be much more sensible than I am, and I would feel almost as insecure as if I were on my own. And besides, I ... I would always be afraid that you might forget me for other girls.' She bit her bottom lip and looked at him with her slyest expression.

'Oh no, you need never be afraid of that!' he said, flattered.

He had forgotten to pay heed to her fatal little 'if'.

'Yes, and it's much better like this,' she went on. 'Because now I have someone old and wise, who can be a support for me. And although no one believes me, it's a fact that I do want so terribly to be wise and not be silly like so many girls. I see enough of all that at school, believe me!'

'I am sure you will turn out a good little wife in time.'

'Yes, you know, I feel I really do want to,' she said confidingly. 'I do so want to be nice to everyone, but sometimes all the wild old tricks come into my mind, and then I can't control myself, but invent new bits of mischief. And if I get scolded, I turn nasty; because I can be like that sometimes, but then – you see – I go very *quiet*.'

'Oh, I could never be cross with you,' he said warmly.

'Couldn't you? Why then, I'm sure I shall grow fond of you. Because somehow, I sometimes feel so alone, as if no-one cared for me, and as if the whole world would carry on just as well if I didn't exist – and it's such an empty feeling. And then I wish that someone was really fond of me, fonder of me than of anyone else. Not because we are relations or anything, but truly for my own sake, and I could tell them everything. It really is so dull going around thinking and thinking and never having anyone to tell about it all. And there are times, Paul, when I feel so sad I can't stop myself from crying, although I don't know what for, and I feel such a longing – such a *terrible* longing.'

She stopped short and looked doubtfully down at the trimming on her dress. He raised her hand and kissed it.

And then she pulled her chair up to his, so they were sitting side by side, and she turned to him, leaning forward and resting her elbows on his knee. Then she looked up into his face. He took her hands in his, and they sat in silence for a while.

'I've got Papa, of course, as you know,' she said, 'but he's always so confoundedly busy with his business affairs, and anyway it isn't *that*. Can you be fond of me?' It was she who asked the question, not he.

But he answered her enquiry by smiling and squeezing her hands, and his earlier desire gradually gave way to a mysterious power, to something warm and caressing, like when you are sitting by the fire one evening, and a couple of little lads – snuggled up on your lap – rest their heads against you, enjoying the silence in peace, enjoying the dark and their own trust. The Squire had never felt that, never even imagined it, so although what he experienced was something like that feeling, he did not understand it.

And so a certain melancholy came into the atmosphere, an aching, puzzling melancholy, as if they both felt sorry for someone, but who ... who?

At that moment, the Rector opened the door. He stood on the threshold for a moment, surveying the tableau.

The Squire was sitting in a high-backed chair, and only the upper part of the back of his head was visible above it.

Selma was the main figure. With the lighting of a Rembrandt, the glow of the lamp fell on her fair hair and the wilful lines of her profile; everything else remained in shadow. But in her very position as she leant over and in the way she had thrown back her head there was a devoted expression which caused the Rector a stabbing discomfort, like an electric shock.

For a moment, he could not ward off a sense of the perversity of things, and it suddenly struck him that over there he should have been glimpsing some other head than Paul Kristerson's. The thought of his son flashed momentarily into his mind. How would it have felt to see the two of them sitting there?

They were so close to him, those two. For them he had planned, on them he had pinned his hopes. It was so natural to wish for their union! He felt a passing weakness. But no. A long engagement and a marriage of cousins – it was not to his taste, and a failing business ... perhaps ... and debts? No.

He smiled at his fancy, a dry, ironic smile. No, they should make their way in the world, both he and she. Money is power. He – the assistant rector's son, who had starved and fawned his way through his examinations – he knew.

He gave a few coughs and went over to them.

'Is everything decided now?' he said genially.

'Yes, it is all decided,' replied the contented fiancé.

'God bless you child, I believe you will make a good wife,' said the Rector.

Touched by his tone of voice, Selma flew up and threw her arms around his neck. As she pressed herself to him, he felt a long, trembling sigh. It was her last, resigned farewell to working for her own future, and he had to steel himself against it as if against the pangs of conscience.

'Now I shall go and inform my good lady,' he said, 'although I strongly suspect that she already has some inkling, as I have noted that she is desperately busy organizing things down in the kitchen.'

But Selma still clung to him.

'And I shall telegraph your father this very evening. You may be sure he will be glad.' He whispered it in her ear, slowly and softly.

Then she looked up into his face; it was rejuvenated by a kindly, contented smile.

As her uncle kissed her forehead and left the room with an encouraging nod, she felt as pleased with herself as if she had done a good deed. And in exuberant delight she rushed over to her fiancé and began to walk beside him, up and down.

It felt so good to hang onto his arm, playful and wilful, and talk about all manner of things, while he listened with a good-natured interest, in his most winning way. Her self-deception presented her with a lie, a distorted picture that looked very much like happiness.

The Squire suddenly stopped and looked at his fiancée.

There may be quite a few items you would like to have,' he said, 'but if I go off and buy you all sorts of things, I may not choose the right ones.'

She looked up at him, happy and carefree, without quite understanding his meaning.

What the Squire felt, as he looked into her trusting face, exceeded his wildest expectations. For it was something quite new, something he had never experienced before. It was something like gratitude. And since for him there was only *one* way of expressing this, he took out his wallet.

She stood and watched, curious and interested. Now they had no secrets from each other; what fun!

'It will be best if you buy what you want yourself,' he said, leafing through the banknotes. There were quite a lot of them, for he had decided in advance that it 'costs' to be engaged. 'Look – shall we say three hundred kronor to start with?'

She kept hold of his arm, but drew as far away from him as she could.

He waved the notes to indicate that she should take them.

'I mean for absolutely anything you want, of course,' he said, smiling at her look. 'I shall be buying the engagement presents myself.'

She shook her head and put her hand behind her back, as if she were afraid to touch the notes.

He laughed. How childish she still was! But he liked her all the better for it.

'Don't you want to?'

'No. I'm sure Uncle will give me all I need.' She looked unshakeably earnest.

He found it hard to suppress his laughter, but put away his money.

'As you wish,' he said.

They resumed their stroll, but she was not as merry as before.

Just then, Mrs Berg came in. She was red from the heat of the kitchen, and perhaps with emotion, too. Her eyes were sharp, but she gave a courteous smile as she offered her congratulations. It was plain that she was making an effort to be pleasant.

They sat down to dine. The groom-to-be next to the hostess, his fiancée next to the host. The conversation was lively, thanks to the Rector, who was unusually cheerful. He asked for wine to be brought, and the maid who was serving at table looked at Selma with a knowing curiosity. In addition, she waited on her with an attentive respect that by no means escaped its object. This heightened the festive atmosphere. The lady of the house was the epitome of politeness, but had the look of a sacrificial lamb. She could not forget the injustice of allowing this child, 'who hadn't the slightest idea', to manage servants and an estate. It felt like an insult ... These new times with their principles of equality – God preserve us – where will it all end?

Anything that was not to her taste she tended to put down to the new times; and many things were not, for she suffered from chronic indigestion.

They talked of announcing the engagement as soon as the rings had been bought.

'And I shall arrange for the announcement in the newspaper straight away,' said the groom-to-be.

'If I may be allowed to express *my* opinion,' said the lady of the house, 'cards are so much more refined. This new fashion for ...'

'But this is more radical,' insisted the Squire.

'Yes, we shall have it in the paper,' announced Selma decisively. She did it with a certain malicious pleasure: now her aunt would not dare to correct her.

Her fiancé nodded to her across the table. He found it quite in order that she took his side; it improved his opinion of her intelligence.

'Announcements in the newspapers have a great future in every respect,' he said, 'just wait and see, Mrs Berg, soon people will even be advertising for marriage partners.'

'Oh, but you cannot be in earnest,' answered the lady.

'Why not? I consider it a very practical arrangement.'

'Surely you don't mean it?' cried Selma, looking a little shocked.

'Indeed I do. Why will it not do as well for that as for anything else?'

A strange repugnance came over her at his words. There was something outrageous in them, she felt; but she could find no word or thought for the sensation – only disgust.

It was as if his assertion degraded *her* – as if it implied something that she should be ashamed of. But she could not work out quite what it was.

'It's wrong,' she said quickly.

'Oh no, it can never be wrong,' her fiancé contradicted her, 'because if a marriage is lawful, it is no-one's business how the parties became acquainted. That is a private matter.'

'But to advertise for a wife! Can you know in advance that you will like a person you have never seen?'

'There is no way of determining that in advance; one would naturally have to tread carefully.'

Selma made no answer, but cast her uncle a look of appeal.

'I do not consider it appropriate, but it can never be called wrong,' was his response.

'But it's ... it's ... ,' she searched for the word, 'it's disgusting.'

'I would go so far as to agree with you, Selma,' said Mrs Berg.

Selma gave her a grateful look, and the Rector changed the subject. However, a sense of gloom had come over her; she was amiable enough, but the cheerfulness had gone.

The rest of the evening passed slowly, but the Squire was delighted anyway.

When the time came for him to leave, he went into the Rector's room on the pretext of lighting a cigar. The Rector realized that there was something he wanted to say.

'I would like to make one request,' said the Squire, 'and that is to be allowed to leave this money with you, and if there is anything Selma wants, then ... '

The Squire took out his three hundred kronor again. They were burning a hole in his pocket. He was so used to paying for everything in cash, and this was a debt of honour, he felt.

'I have promised her ... ' The Rector gave a modest cough.

'Yes, she mentioned it, and absolutely refused to accept anything, but what I thought, was ... Well, it would give me such pleasure, you see. She need never find out.'

The Rector patted him on the shoulder. 'I quite understand,' he said, looking a little touched. 'You can rest assured that the child will get everything she wants.'

And on that note they parted.

Chapter 5

The engagement period did not pass without discord, with the Squire himself referring to it as 'a seething ebb and flow', although it was hard to imagine why, as he was mostly received with indifference. The result, however, was that he brought the wedding forward as far as he possibly could.

The Squire was to move to his new property before the marriage, so that everything could be made ready for its mistress. Mrs Berg provided the guiding principle in all the arrangements, and their shared concerns turned her and the Squire into bosom friends, for he had one great merit, that splendid habit of never worrying how much a thing cost, as long as it looked good and was for his own benefit.

Selma, too, rose in the worthy lady's estimation, for she left all the arrangements to them, and whenever they asked what she thought, she would always answer: 'Fine.' If there was more indifference than approval in the answer, it mattered little. But more than once, she asked her fiancé to release her from her promise. She did not want to break off the engagement against his wishes, bound as she was by her high-flown ideas of the claims of honour and the sacred nature of a promise.

She possessed a certain romantic 'chivalry', despite being a woman – or perhaps for that very reason.

The negotiations always ended, however, with her merely regretting that she had distressed such a Job of patience. His unprecedented willingness to be accommodating had more effect than anything else. So she gradually found herself in a calmer and more trusting frame of mind. There were times when she was even happy and loving. Then the Squire felt he wanted to buy her the whole world.

The days leading up to the wedding passed in undisturbed harmony. She felt completely confident: she could twist him around her little finger.

At the rectory, there was a tremendous bustle and no peace from the wedding preparations. Mrs Berg was one of those housewives who do not miss a single opportunity to turn the house upside down – naturally with constant laments about the disruption they themselves have caused.

For the Rector, who loved peace and quiet, it was a trying time, but he kept to his rooms and rejoiced in his victory.

The wedding was to take place on the twentieth of November. That was not far off, but then there was no reason to delay. Their first thought had been to wait until the bride's seventeenth birthday, but then the wedding would have come in the middle of all the Christmas preparations, and three weeks more or less made little difference.

But as the bride put it herself, 'It is very silly to be just sixteen, though'.

The bridegroom had talked of a simple wedding, with light refreshments, and of leaving straight afterwards, but Mrs Berg would not hear of it. This was to be a proper wedding, with lots of guests. The Rector let her have her way; he always did when it was a matter to which he attached little weight himself.

On the morning of the all-important day, Selma was shut away in one of the guest rooms, for no-one was to see her before the ceremony. Those were Mrs Berg's strict instructions, and Selma was more than happy to follow them, since her head was covered in curl-papers, which stuck out in all directions and were not at all becoming.

Her place of detention was a large room with rickety furniture and a single window.

To begin with, she amused herself by rearranging all the splendours of the bridal gown, which had been laid out on the sofa. But eventually she tired of it, and began to long for liberation.

Thanks to the little gold watch her fiancé had given her, she at least had the consolation of seeing how time was going by. But she despaired at how slowly it was passing.

The sound of a carriage made her jump to her feet. Guests from the station, Papa for sure – perhaps Richard too! She could see nothing, for the window faced the garden.

Richard had written to say that it would be impossible for him to come, and he had only promised to do so at his father's express insistence. But perhaps he still wouldn't come! That would be just like him – always at odds with everyone.

Sulkily, she put her elbows on the table and rested her head in her hands; the curl-papers made it feel so lumpy. What if she took one of them out to see how it would look? But no, it would only lose its curl. Her cold hands clasped her forehead; it was aching inside.

How peculiar all these thoughts were! It seemed to her as though they were moving over a thin surface, which could only just support them at this point, but which must eventually break. She tried hard to keep them all together, but they scattered like frightened sheep. Oh, if only they would keep still – quite still. That was the only right thing to do. For now they could not anticipate events a single hour ahead without encroaching into forbidden territory. That was for her what is known as 'purity of mind'; that was the grand total of the principles she had been given to guide her through life, or rather as far as the altar – for they extended no further. And she would have despised herself, had she secretly pondered questions that she would have been ashamed to articulate. She was such an honourable little soul.

She would have liked to read through the marriage service now, if she had had a hymnbook, for she was not wholly familiar with it: people laughed at girls who learnt it by heart. It was somehow shameful. But she would make her responses loud and clear, anyway.

Paul had asked her not to cry. Pooh, what was there to cry for! It was supposed to be a joyful occasion, after all. Hm. Only moderately joyful, it seemed to her

She heard footsteps, out in the corridor – they must be Richard's! She rushed to the door and opened it a crack. Just enough to listen but not be seen.

'Richard!'

She said it quietly and shyly, but her tone of her voice revealed something of her delight and expectation. He could say something to her, even if they were not allowed to see each other. It had been an eternity since they had last seen each other, and he hadn't even congratulated her.

But no answer came, only the sound of footsteps moving away.

'Richard!'

This time the word contained disappointment and reproach.

But the steps had already departed, and she heard a door close.

'I'm sure it was him, just the same,' she grumbled, and went back to her place. For a moment, the urge to cry knotted her throat, but she mastered it.

At last, Karna the dressmaker came in with dinner on a tray.

'They all send their best wishes,' she said.

'Is Papa there?'

'Yes.'

'And Richard?'

'Yes.'

Karna moved the toilet mirror to one side and put the tray down on the table.

'Poor young lady, having to sit in here!'

'Ugh, yes! I think I shall be bored to death.'

'And we're rushed off our feet, Miss. The drawing-room decorations are nearly done, and it's looking so lovely.'

'Mm?'

'Yes indeed. But our young student's going about glaring like a hungry dog.'

'Why?'

'That I don't know.'

'Is anyone else there?'

'Yes, a few guests who came on the train.'

Karna was about to go.

'Dear Karna, come to dress me in good time, so at least I have something to do.'

'As soon as everything's done in the drawing room.'

And Karna went.

Once Selma had finished her meal, she began the preparations for her toilette, to while away the time. There was a knock at the door.

'Who is it?'

'It's me, darling,' replied the bridegroom.

'You're not to come in!'

'No, I know. I just wanted to say something to you.'

She ran to the door and took hold of the handle to make sure.

'What did you want to say?'

'I'm going to give Karna a little something, and I would like you to wear it today. It is my gift to the bride.'

'Thank you, thank you. I wonder what it can be.'

'Do you want to see?'

'Oh yes! Pass it to me.'

It was like an emergency anchor: something on which to fix her thoughts. She opened the door only as far as she thought necessary, and stood aside so she would not be seen. He passed her a little box, and she shut the door.

With a little pressure from her finger, the lid opened.

'But Paul, what is it?'

'A brooch,' he said with a laugh.

'No, I mean the stones.'

'Diamonds.'

That was what she had suspected as soon as she saw them sparkling against the velvet lining. That was why her heart had begun to race.

'Real diamonds?'

'Yes, real ones.'

'O-hh.'

That was all she said, but it expressed so much, that he felt himself amply rewarded.

She sat down over by the window and looked at her treasure. She held it first in the shadow, then in the light, to see which made it glitter the most. After that she tried it in front of the mirror, first against the linen of her peignoir, then amongst the curl-papers in her hair. Oh, it was exquisite!

Before she knew it, the dressmaker was there to dress her.

'Look, Karna!' she cried, holding out the brooch, 'I'm to wear this.'

'But Miss,' objected Karna earnestly, 'You should never wear something like that on your wedding day, it's a bad omen. You should only wear myrtle.'

'Oh well, I've already promised my fiancé that I will,' said Selma impatiently. She did not feel the least inclined to part with her latest toy. While the dressmaker took out the curl papers, she sat motionless before the mirror, with two red patches burning on her cheeks, as they always did when she was impatient for something.

'Now the mistress can come and put your crown on,' said Karna at last, inspecting her masterpiece, the white satin dress, and draping the train across the floor to its full extent. Selma stood stiff and strained, hardly daring to move in all her finery, but feeling pleased with it nonetheless.

Her aunt came in, together with several female relations, all in silk and baubles. Selma had to sit down, for she was taller than Mrs Berg, and then her crown was fastened in place, nestling deep in the froth of her veil. Her aunt kissed her on the forehead and cried, the others squeezed her hand and cried. Selma felt as if they were about to bury her, and tears rose to sicken her again, although she knew it was stupid.

She looked around in indignation, fighting back her tears.

'If you're going to blub, you might at least not do it in here,' she said fiercely. She had promised Paul not to cry.

They left her alone, and she was calm again. Oh yes, one more thing: she wanted to look Selma Berg in the face, one last time. She bent forward and looked in the mirror.

Was it really her? The glossy curls, falling over her shoulders, the crown above the carefully set hair of her fringe, and this gossamer tulle, enveloping her like a cloud – it was all so new – so enchantingly new!

Her father came to fetch her – so emotional that he could not speak.

'Be strong, Papa,' she said, and put her hand in his. It was trembling violently, and she felt the irritation rise in her again. What was all this? Were they all conspiring to make a cry-baby of her?

They walked along the carpeted corridor, which was dim in spite of the bracket lamps on the walls. Not a footfall could be heard, not a word was said, and the anxious shaking passed from her father's hand to hers. And all at once it came over her – everything she had wanted to suppress – a suffocating uncertainty, an inexplicable dread.

Was she on her way to the altar or the scaffold? Oh God! ... – I don't believe in Him, so He will punish me – There it was again, the old paradox! Was the punishment about to come?

Black spots flickered before her eyes, and a treacherous weakness crept into her limbs.

The double doors were thrown open, and they entered the drawing room, where a dazzling light met them. She sensed all eyes fixed on her and did not dare to lift her own. The black spots dancing before them grew larger and larger, and she felt a strange chill in the pit of her stomach.

Summoning all her self-control, she subdued the trembling of her lips, and diffidently and gravely took her place at the bridegroom's side before the altar, where her uncle, book in hand, stood ready to unite their destinies for life and call down the blessing of God on their lawful union.

The service began, and the ladies sobbed gently into their handkerchiefs, but without taking their eyes off the bride for a single second.

And she ... she had no thought for anything but those flickering black spots, which told her that prolonging this torture by even a minute would be enough to make her collapse onto the carpet in a faint. Tonelessly, but without faltering, she repeated the vows read out to her, and the whole marriage service ran so faultlessly that not the slightest hint of a criticism could be made – except of the frightening pallor of the bride.

And a bride without tears! ... the more elderly of the ladies shook their heads.

As Selma accepted congratulations, she could hardly keep upright, but her deportment was impeccable. The oppressive anxiety that had descended on her had brought with it a new self-awareness. Her instinct for self-preservation taught her to hide her state of mind from those curious looks. She did not forget for a moment how her train should be draped, how her veil should lie, how her bouquet should be held. The very tone of her voice was carefully judged, her smile was deliberate, and those eyes with their modest gratitude – their expression was as well calculated as if she had practised it in front of her mirror a hundred times.

She felt as if she had entered into the existence of someone else, totally alien to her. She moved as if in a dream, yet with complete control, every nerve taut.

Was she a prisoner among enemies? Were their eyes spying out for the slightest sign that she was suffering? Oh, never, never! ... And so she smiled on them all with that placid smile, which sent the ladies into raptures at how 'pretty' she was. But inside her, that terrible uncertainty went on gnawing.

Everyone was so kind, so deferential, almost pitying. Everyone except the Squire, who was beaming and happy – everyone except Richard, who seemed to have become a stranger to her. Of the cousin, the friend, the sparring partner, there was now not a sign. He was a polite young man, who answered when she addressed him; that was all. But it was also the straw that almost broke the camel's back.

Selma went over to a window by herself and looked out. She must take a free breath or perish, she felt.

The blinds had not been let down, for the courtyard was swarming with parishioners wanting to see what a wedding at the rectory was like. The flaring torches cast a fantastical light on the figures moving about down there.

Selma shaded her eyes to get a better look. What was that? Yes it was ... Old Mother Möller! She was gripped by a wild joy and her heart started pounding. Axel was up in the house, he had been invited for Richard's sake – and now his mother was here

77

too! She positioned herself in such a way that she was bound to be noticed from down there. Just then, the Rector came over to her.

'Uncle, shall we go downstairs to the parish office and let the people see us?' she said quickly. 'The courtyard is full, and they can't see anything of us here.'

'That is just what I was going to ask you to do,' replied the Rector, who was a populist.

And down they went, surrounded by young ladies with bouquets and young gentlemen with candelabras. It made a fine bridal procession. Selma took her husband's arm and stood in the centre of the room, adjusting her train with her foot. She wanted to be properly inspected.

The crowd cheered.

But the bride's gaze was searching out one particular face – one pointed nose and two sharp eyes. There! ... but over in the shadows, so she was scarcely visible. For a moment, the child's face in the bridal veil bore an ugly old smile, cold and spiteful.

Revelling in Old Mother Möller's envy allowed Selma to forget her anxiety. A cheeky look came into her eyes, and she shifted slightly, knowing it would make the diamonds sparkle. That would be one in the eye for a certain person! She could hardly stop herself laughing out loud. Now she was richer than Old Mother Möller, richer than Jöns Ols' Marie. Now they could look her up and down if they cared to. And she moved her glossy satin train out to one side, so they would see how long it was.

Then she turned regally, and they returned to the party upstairs, with the cheers of the crowd resounding outside.

'I've given instructions for them all to be served a little something,' said the Squire. He was delighted by the noisy tribute.

The supper was superb, but seemed to go on for ever. Or so it seemed to Selma. She could not eat, and felt ready to collapse with exhaustion. The mental strain had drained her resources. Everything had stormed in on her at once, and it had been too much even for her strong constitution.

In one corner of the drawing room stood Axel Möller,

devouring mushroom vol-au-vent, pale as a ghost.

The more he drank, the paler he became.

Selma had seen his spectacles glinting in her direction all evening, from one corner or another. But now he seemed to have forgotten her for his vol-au-vent. She did not care, either way. She was so tired, so tired! If only it would end!

Now Richard was going over to speak to Axel. He looked grave, almost angry. She wondered what he could have to say, but she could not make out a word, since they were in the opposite corner.

'Axel, you've had enough to drink.'

Richard's manner was always abrupt, but this evening it was worse than usual.

'At a wedding, you need to quench your thirst,' replied Axel in his thin voice, with a little laugh.

'You're not allowed to have a thirst,' continued Richard. 'And what's more, you've taken every opportunity to quench it already. I've had my eye on you.'

'I've drunk no more than you,' replied Axel, trying to laugh but producing a short, hollow cough.

'With your constitution, I'd give it up too,' said the student. 'But why have you changed your tune? I mean, you were a teetotaller.'

'Changed my tune! What do you mean by that? Because just for once I ... '

'Now come on, don't pretend. I know very well that you're familiar with the back way into Slätticke Inn. You see I've been kept well informed.'

Axel gave such a start that Richard had to put a calming hand on his arm.

'Since when have you been my guardian?'

'I'm not your guardian, but I am a doctor.'

'With nothing but an exam in philosophy of medicine to your name !'

'That makes no difference, since I know what I'm talking about. Stop it now. I wouldn't have brought it up this evening, but I leave tomorrow morning, so we won't be seeing each other again.'

'Don't worry.'

'But you'll do as I say?'

Richard gave him a straight, sharp look, and he averted his eyes.

'It's all the same,' said Axel in a different tone of voice.

'What is?'

'Everything.'

'Don't talk nonsense!'

Then the Rector tapped his glass, interrupting their conversation.

By the end of the toasts, Axel had disappeared. Richard looked in vain for him in every room.

He waited half an hour, and then began his search anew. He finally found him down in the cloakroom, sitting on his own by a lamp, writing in his notebook.

'My dear fellow, why are you sitting here?'

'Don't you think I'm in better company here than up there among all that chatter? Do you think I would want to change places with a single one of you?' He threw himself back in the chair and regarded his friend with an inspired smile. His spectacles glittered in the lamplight.

'You're a hopeless dreamer. What are you up to this time?' There was a certain desperation in Richard's tone.

'See for yourself!' Axel threw the book onto the table among a heap of shawls.

His friend picked it up with a dark look.

'Some people are destined to live short but intense lives,' said Axel, with a toss of the head.

'Intense?' repeated his friend. 'You mean lunatic. That would be nearer the truth.'

'We won't argue about what to call it.'

'So – you write poetry?'

'Better people than I have done it.'

'And done it better than you – no doubt.'

'Posterity will be the judge of that.'

Richard did not answer, but turned his head as if to appeal to someone.

Then he looked in the book.

'No, you mustn't read it!' cried Axel suddenly, leaping up and grabbing it from him.

Their eyes met for a second, but not a word was said. Then Richard left him.

After he had gone, the poet opened his book once more and read in a whisper what he had written after many crossings out:

> May I not hate? You craven race,
> Chill piety, bid your teachings hide,
> Awoken by Destiny's rough embrace,
> Whose powers remain by you untried.
> You think yourself warm, if your ice is turning
> To melted tears which reluctantly flow;
> Dried by red-hot torment, mine are burning,
> My silent suffering you cannot know.
>
> Fool! For faith and hope you still find room,
> When the parting clouds reveal the sun,
> But your joy may never reach full bloom
> Once fate with the breaking of stems is done.
> I too had faith which came to nought,
> My hopes to hopeless shreds are torn.
> My youth, ambition, all to ruin brought,
> Yielding a harvest of thistle and thorn.
>
> No heavenly angels guide my way,
> Black spirits my hapless self have driven:
> In angry waves and surging spray,
> My helpless ship is lost and riven.
> Then all at once new hope appeared
> - a beacon's light shone from afar -
> To sharp and hidden rocks my course I steered:
> Deception lay in that false bright star.
>
> So I will hate the hand which lit

That lamp to obscure my shadowy goal!
But defy the power by which I am hit
With this agony deep in my soul!
What matters it if cold I lie
When my only remaining desire must be -
To see once again before I die,
That falsest star. – She is dear to me!'

He could feel his pulse throbbing and his head burning. Yes, fame would come – in spite of everything, for Sweden had found itself a new Lidner; he was sure of it now.

*

On the second day of the wedding, there was to be a late family breakfast at the rectory, and in the evening a supper dance at the home of the newly-weds.

When Selma awoke that morning, she lay there for a long time, just thinking.

The winter morning cast its dull grey light through the curtains, heavy – like a look incapable of lifting its eyelids. Her eyes moved to the wedding dress, hanging over a chair by the window. The veil lay discarded and crumpled, the crown had been damp and had left nasty, greenish stains on it. Its end was in tatters, turned a dusty, dirty grey by floors and staircases.

It was so like her own mood.

It was the same feeling she had had when the Squire talked about advertising for a bride, the only difference being that it was now more definite – not mere suspicion, but knowledge.

The room felt cold, and she wished there were a fire. It would have brought a little cheer.

He had told her that was what people were like – all of them. And what of her, then? A sense of disgust came over her. In the whole world, there was nothing of all she had dreamt of – nothing! Lies, lies, the whole thing! – fairytales for children, that they tricked you into believing and then forced you to forget.

An unrelenting succession of questions came sweeping in on

her, screaming for answers, as voracious as starving vultures. But where could she find answers to them all? Only now, now that she had the right to think, could she see how many there were.

And why had she not had that right until now?

She sat up in bed and pushed the hair back from her face with both hands. It was not plaited, but wild and loose like a lion's mane; still curly, but tangled and matted in its extravagant profusion.

She looked about her for a clock, but there was none in the room. Then she threw a glance at the other bed. A fleeting look, but one from which she did not seem free to tear away her eyes at will.

Was this the man she had been married to yesterday? It seemed to her that she had never seen him before.

Selma stared at the face of a stranger, and her body trembled; her teeth chattered.

Yesterday, she had almost thought him good-looking. His huge frame looked well in black, and his stately bearing had enhanced the ceremonial air of his attire. In his manner there was at times a hint of refinement, and to that had been added yesterday such a look of bliss, that it had lent his whole face an air of youth and intelligence.

But now it looked colossal, that head, lying there on the embroidered pillow, framed with coquettish lace. And Selma found that Hercules neck appalling. She stared at its strong sinews, swollen veins and rough skin. And then that enormous face, lying there so vacuous and coarse, with no sign of life but the breath rhythmically bubbling out through the thick purplish lips.

Love him? ... love, honour and keep him, in sickness and in health. Oh God ...

The noise of a door in the distance finally brought her back to herself and to the fact that it was the second day of her wedding, that there would be visitors and fuss today too, and that she would have to endure all those looks, just as she had yesterday.

Footsteps were approaching. The maid was coming to make

the fire. Was she to see him like this?

Selma stretched over and shook him by the arm.

'What is it?' he said peevishly, and opened his eyes.

At that moment, the maid came in.

Then he woke up properly, and when he saw Selma, his face grew animated.

'Good morning, wife,' he said cheerily, holding out his large hand.

She shook the hand and smiled – for the sake of the maid. With this action she inaugurated the first day of her married life. And then she put on her new, elegant morning gown, ready to make her appearance with the dignity of a young married woman.

Everything irreproachably correct.

Breakfast was animated and the bride cheerful. The only one who seemed out of spirits was Richard. He was to leave after the meal. It was 'impossible' for him to stay any longer, and the Rector did not feel inclined to insist.

His leave-taking was hurried and cold.

'Goodbye Selma,' he said, 'Good luck.'

Not a hint of cordiality. Nothing.

Selma went over to one of the windows to watch as he climbed into the carriage. Her forehead was burning and her throat felt constricted. If she could only be allowed to weep ... weep – uncontrollably! ...

She leant her head against the window frame. No-one could see her face. But Richard did not turn round – just busied himself with the travelling rug. Not a single look! He used to be abrupt, but never like this; this was a deliberate snub.

The carriage moved off. He raised his hat without looking up.

An arm was placed around Selma's shoulders. It was the Rector. She looked up into his face. Was it possible! – was he fighting back tears too? She put her arms around his neck and kissed him. The desire to give comfort made her forget her own sorrow. Encouragingly she stroked his dark, sleeked-down hair with her hand, just as she used to do with her father, when he was unhappy.

At this, a slightly sorrowful look crept over the Rector's controlled features. Perhaps at this moment he needed her kindliness more than anyone else.

But his weakness only lasted for a moment.

Before long, the carriages were brought round. They were all to travel together to the home of the newly-wed couple, thirty kilometres away; the Rector had arranged for the visiting relations to accompany them there, and then to travel back in the evening. He wished there to be no farewells until everything was over. Selma might get very upset – she was so unpredictable – and he did not want any unnecessary witnesses.

As they drew up at the foot of the steps to the large, two-storey house, the Squire jumped down from the carriage and helped Selma out.

'Welcome to your own home,' he said, and kissed her.

She felt herself give a start at the words. Everything was so new and strange. Even her footsteps sounded so odd on the smooth flagstone floor. There was nothing in this great house that was hers. It was his – all his! She felt like a scrounger, and when the maid curtsied, shook her hand and said: 'Good-day ma'am', she felt thoroughly ashamed. What right had she to be here?

'Go in, child,' said Mrs Berg, who had by now also dismounted from the carriage.

'You first, Aunt,' replied Selma, moving aside.

'Hm, acting the hostess already, I see,' answered her aunt a little sourly. She took it for conceit.

Selma blushed, and tears pricked her eyes. Her father came up.

'God bless your going out and your coming in,' he said, in his gentle, melodic voice.

She gave him a hug of genuine affection, smiling as she looked into his face, where moods and expressions changed as swiftly as in a child's.

Now she was happy again. After all, *he* was positively beaming at all this splendour, and he had still only seen the outside. What a surprise it would be for him!

She pulled him into the hall, where they took off their furs.

There was much chatter and commotion. The air was cold and raw, and it was so nice to come into the warm.

Then coffee was served. And afterwards it was time to take a tour and examine everything. Gasps of admiration could be heard wherever they went. It was all so new, so comfortable and attractive.

The Squire took Selma through the kitchens and outbuildings, and all the servants were introduced to the new mistress, who felt awfully embarrassed by their curious stares, which seemed to echo her own assertion that 'it is very silly to be just sixteen'. But she tried her very hardest to maintain her dignity.

The housekeeper was a mature person, who looked kind and was new to the job. Selma started getting to know her at once, and felt that here at least was someone to keep her company in her new home.

When it was time to change, the Squire himself had to remind Selma. She was touring the rooms, holding her father's arm and delighting in his enthusiasm.

At times she had to laugh out loud at his naïveté, when they encountered some innovation whose use he could not fathom.

'Well, I must go and change now,' she said, withdrawing her hand from his arm. 'But I do hope you will do your necktie really elegantly, and not come looking all untidy. Because I'm afraid *I* won't have time to help you today,' she added. That was her punch line. She looked at him again. He was such a dear, her Papa! His head was as white as a dove's, although he was only just out of his forties.

He just chuckled. She ruffled his hair for a moment, before she ran off. It was silky and wavy; it had always been a delight for her to make free with that hair.

How she liked the old child! She paused at the door to blow him a kiss.

Her trunk stood in the bedroom, and she hurried to unpack it. This was turning out to be fun after all! She shook out her skirts one by one as she took them out. And the dress ... it certainly was elegant. Could one imagine a lovelier colour than that delicate blue, so soft, such a treat for the eye, with those silver threads shimmering through it!

And what a funny sensation when your feet touched the softness of the carpets and seemed to sink into them! If she could only get it into her head that it was hers ... her very own! But she could not. That these carpets were just as much hers as the cow-hair matting at home at the rectory was her aunt's. At home? It had never occurred to her before that there was something so nice and warm about the very word, something which makes you want to say it more than once and rest on it, as it were, put your ear right up against it and listen, as if for the sound of a well-known note.

But what was wrong with Richard? If only he had been here this evening! No doubt she would have managed to cheer him up in the end, after all.

He used to say that she never looked so 'human' as when she was wearing blue. *Used to* say? – She gave a laugh. Well, actually he hadn't said it more than once, and that was that day ... just think, so long ago! ... why, it was that summer he had come to visit her and Papa. It was just after he got his place as a student. He was certainly much more pleasant then than he had been recently.

And as she thought all this, she attended to the details of her toilette. Once she had on her pale blue shoes and her long underskirt, she strutted to and fro across the floor, looking backwards over her naked shoulder down at the ornamented train. How frightfully smart she looked!

Just then, her husband came in. She gave a squeal and covered herself with her peignoir. Then he laughed at her and said there was no need. And she blushed furiously and made haste to put on her dress and get out into the drawing-room. The mirror was better there, she said.

Shortly afterwards, the guests began to arrive. There were interminable introductions, for Selma was not acquainted with many of them. But they were all so amiable that she soon felt she knew them.

She particularly liked one matronly lady who – attired in a

dress of heavy silk – came sailing into the room with a workbag over her arm. She had such a good-natured little double chin, and there was a kind but roguish look in her eyes.

The Squire received her with the greatest respect and Selma gave a deep curtsey.

'Oh, what wickedness, this is a mere child,' she said with a laugh, stroking Selma's cheek. 'When my daughters reach your age, I shall keep them to pigtails and satchels.'

Selma felt a strong urge to throw her arms round the lady's neck for this wise comment, but had to content herself with appearing flattered. After all, she was a married woman now.

It goes without saying that Selma was the life and soul of the party.

She danced until she almost dropped, the blood rushed to her head, her heart pounded. The music, the lights, the compliments – everything conspired to make her feel utterly light-headed.

The Squire was dancing too. He really looked quite a fine figure again today.

Selma stood watching him as she took a rest. How superbly he led! How was it possible for such bulk to carry itself so lightly?

She gave a sudden start. She remembered something. What was that tale her old nursemaid used to tell her?

King Lindworm was the most stately of lords, powerful and rich. At his wedding, he made his Queen promise that she would never enter his chamber while he slept, for it would cause them both great misfortune. She loved him very much, and would have promised him greater things than that, had he asked. They lived happily together, for as long as the Queen kept her promise.

But one day her curiosity got the better of her. At midnight, she took a candle and crept to the King's bedchamber. There she saw him lying on the bed, coiled up – a scaly monster – and the sight of him horrified and frightened her so much, that her feet could hardly carry her from the place.

Now her curiosity was satisfied.

But she could never forget that sight, and each time King Lindworm took her in his arms, it was as if he resumed the form

88

of the scaly monster, so slithery and cold that his embrace made her writhe in agony.

So then their love was dead and, grieve as they might, it could never be brought back to life.

Selma shivered, as if a nocturnal wind had swept through the room. But she felt she could have loved King Lindworm even more – for the promise he had demanded.

It was time for the guests to depart. They said their goodnights and the rooms emptied.

The Squire and Selma stood side by side as their guests slowly filed out. The Squire was in rather high spirits.

'Do you know what that fool Bergstrand said to me yesterday evening on his way out?' he asked.

'No.'

The Squire bent down and whispered something in her ear; then burst out laughing.

Selma flushed crimson and bit her lip. Yesterday, she would not even have understood.

Now only her father and her aunt and uncle were left. Selma went up to them.

'Now it is our turn to say farewell,' began the Rector in his most guarded tone. He hated scenes, and hoped his composure would keep Selma's emotion in check.

Of tears there was no sign, but she seemed agitated, gripped him tightly by the arm and whispered:

'I would rather come home with you. Oh ... Uncle!'

His face like a thundercloud, he took her aside by the window, while the Squire was still on the far side of the room embracing his new-found friend Mrs Berg, whom he honoured with the title 'Mama-in-law'.

'I must remind you of one thing,' said the Rector in a rapid undertone, 'and that is, that whatever happens, and however you act in your new position, yes, even if you are foolish enough to find it unbearable, there is from this day forward *no* other home for you than your husband's house. Remember that. I speak for your father as well as myself.'

Selma felt a numbing sensation inside her at the icy coldness

89

of his words. And at the same time it was as shocking as a physical punishment. Her whole soul cried out for revenge.

She would have given anything to possess at that moment a single little word that could bore into his soul and wedge fast with its ultra-fine, razor-sharp spiral.

And to have exposed herself in that way! ... The fact that he would now know forever her feelings at that moment ... forever have the advantage of her in this knowledge of how weak she had been!

She had kept her eyes down while he spoke. Now she looked up – slowly, with triumphant scorn. And she put her hands on his shoulders, gently – a movement as restrained as one of his own. At that moment there could be no mistaking their kinship.

'I have often wondered just how much you cared for me,' she said. 'Now I know. Thank you for falling into my trap.'

She laughed, showing glittering teeth. It was the most shameless untruth that had ever dared to pass her lips, and she uttered it without so much as blinking.

There was merely a slight quivering of her nostrils, but that was her rage.

Beaten – Uncle – trapped! Oh, she would never have believed it.

She did not look angry, merely gave a metallic-sounding laugh. And she moved away from him with the feeling a young fox must have the first time it has made a foxhound follow a false scent.

The Squire was still standing at the back of the room. She flicked her train aside and leant on his shoulder, softly and as if seeking his approval.

'Have I shed a tear on my wedding day; is it a wrench to leave them all; are you pleased with me?' she cried, raising her hand. It was a gesture rather like the exultation of a Bacchante.

'I adore you,' he whispered back.

From a caryatid, leaning out from the wall and bearing aloft three tulip-shaped lamps, the light fell on that strange grouping.

The silver threads shimmered in the pastel-blue fabric of the dress, and with her brilliant complexion, her feverishly bright eyes, Selma was almost beautiful: the intensity of an inner life heightened by emotion momentarily suffused her whole being, so it seemed to exceed its own boundaries and rise above itself. But that minute's beauty was an exotic flower, brought artificially into bloom and instantly withering, leaving its fruit to ripen.

The naive child had vanished, the honesty had gone, replaced by dissembling and the instinct for survival; the woman was now complete.

The pupil had overtaken her master.

Chapter 6

More than two years had passed. It was spring. Not that the trees were green, but shoots and the first leaves were spurting into growth and all the buds were swelling.

Selma sat alone at her husband's desk, adding up a page in a cashbook. She had a clear hand, a good head for figures, and some business acumen. These had enabled her gradually to promote herself to the rank of private secretary, and it was usual for her husband to lie on the sofa and dictate, while she sat at the desk writing. It was so convenient, and it also seemed to give her pleasure.

This was what gave their life some semblance of fellowship.

Their marriage was considered one of the happiest. Not only by their social circle, but also – more revealingly – by their servants, who never heard them exchange a cross word. She was pleasant towards him, insofar as her stiff manner permitted, and he worshipped her.

Their wealth continued to grow. It would have done so without their needing to lift a finger.

The Squire was often away. There was a steady stream of business matters: endless conferences, audits, agricultural gatherings, railway discussion groups and shareholders' meetings. He had always been drawn to the good life, and now he could indulge his inclinations. The farm steward was a reliable fellow, who could never be accused of any omission, whether or not his master was at home. And as it happened, Squire Kristerson was considered as indispensable on committees as he was at celebration dinners.

In the early days of her married life, Selma had thrown herself into local social life with wild enthusiasm. Her outfits were extravagant, her manner high-spirited. She always mixed with the other young girls, joking and laughing as they did, and was the most tireless dancer of them all.

On the one hand, the Squire was proud of his young wife, who made a great show of her affection for him in company, but on the other, he mistrusted her. He could not have said why, for she did not seem particularly interested in male company. But as soon as she spoke to a young man, he felt an intense uneasiness and if she laughed, it seemed to pierce him to the core, for at home she seldom laughed.

And then the dancing ... that dancing! It tormented him to see her dancing with others. He reserved as many dances on her programme as he could without making himself look ridiculous, and indeed sometimes went so far that the ladies and girls sitting around began to giggle in corners. Selma sensed the atmosphere and felt the shame. The Squire was oblivious: he had eyes and ears for nothing but her. She offered to give up dancing altogether, but he opposed this most emphatically. It would look as though he were a tyrant, if you please! No, she was to dance and amuse herself. She was young.

At one ball they attended, these tensions flared into a big scene, which was talked about in the whole district – an endless source of delight and discussion for all those 'sitting in judgment'. The Squire had noticed that Selma had danced twice in the course of the evening with one young lieutenant who, in the Squire's eyes, was shamelessly good-looking. Just before the end of the ball, the lieutenant approached once more; it was evidently his polka. But just as he was bowing, the Squire rushed up, put his arm around his wife's waist and panted a furious:

'I shall have this dance with my wife.'

It was hopelessly comical.

The lieutenant took offence, the Squire was rude, and Selma was embarrassed by her husband.

To her it felt indescribably belittling that he should expose his weakness to strangers, but worst of all was the insult of being obliged to share his jealousy with an unknown man, who meant absolutely nothing to her, as she meant nothing to him. It was so hateful to hear this dancing partner standing arguing about her and on her behalf, that she felt the disgrace of it could never be erased. She took a fervent dislike to the poor lieutenant himself, who was taking her part with such chivalry that she wished the ground would open and swallow him up.

From that day forward, she was a different person.

She was in any case too self-controlled to speak of her indignation at her husband's actions, and she made no sudden alteration to the temperature of her manner, but he could not fail to notice how it was cooling, slowly and inexorably. It plunged him into despair. He realized that he had committed an act of folly, and was consumed by the desire to make amends.

Gold and presents showered down over Selma, but she received them with as much careless indifference as if she had grown up with stores of treasure to squander. She always thanked him kindly, but as impassively as if he had knelt at her feet for twenty years.

This aroused him further.

He felt as if he could never get beyond courtship with this woman, who never grew any warmer, and seemed merely more absent, the more passionately he pressed her to him.

She could as well have been fifty as twenty.

Her liking for entertainments had vanished, and if politeness required her to attend a party, she always stayed with the matrons. She could sit for hour after hour, listening with the most attentive of expressions to detailed accounts of trivial ailments, complaints about slovenly maids and confidences about the latest gossip. 'Amazingly advanced' children were among the favoured topics. But for those who have neither ailments nor children, all that can grow monotonous in time. Selma thought so – in spite of her look of interest – and she kept away from such social gatherings whenever she could. People noticed, were offended, and seldom invited her.

She was glad of it; she could avoid sitting in drawing rooms, so straight and 'correct', hearing intermittent snatches of dance music and feeling her feet twitch with the urge to join in, as she enunciated every word so calmly and quietly, for fear of betraying how her heart was pounding with envy.

It was better to sit at home.

So she did. The Squire was obliged to go alone. He made a fuss to begin with and said he was sorry she would be without company for so long, but it gradually became a habit. For her, these were sunny interludes. She felt wonderfully free and happy each time the carriage rolled away. Sometimes she would shout and sing in the big, empty rooms, for the sheer joy of listening to her own unmusical voice and revelling in the fact that there was no-one, no-one, within hearing distance – that she was alone, quite alone! She would even dance around on the carpets, hang by her arms from the high doorposts, and get up to a thousand pranks like the wildest of children. And then she would laugh out loud at herself. It was such joyful madness! ... Oh! ... And how she would long for it sometimes, waiting for him to leave.

He had his world and she had hers. What could the two of them have to say to each other?

Gradually this way of living became so familiar that it ran like a well-regulated watch. Month followed month and nothing changed.

There were two things the Squire had given Selma which had made her really happy. One was a horse to ride, the other a paddock. Once she had these, her gymnastic antics became rare, and she threw herself into her new sport with ravenous interest. The Squire even allowed her to go into town and take riding lessons with an old, married cavalry captain of his acquaintance.

Selma was possessed of exceptional perseverance, and was soon such a model horsewoman that the Squire was proud of her. He gave her a colt to break in for herself, and she devoured every book that she could find, Swedish or foreign, on the training of horses.

Such was her life, and she was now nineteen years old.

When she had written down the last figure, she closed the book. She rested her chin in her hands and looked out into the garden. Not a sound was to be heard in the house. She sat still, thinking.

Her wild mood swings had subsided. She was calmer now than she had been before. But how monotonous this life was! She thought of the future – the years stretched ahead. Perhaps she would reach sixty, seventy; she had such a strong constitution.

She felt sick at the thought of all those years. She felt satiated yet empty. Life is so impoverished and flat and wretched! So wholly unlike what one imagines when one is young.

Young? Was that then no longer what she was?

She raised her eyebrows and adopted a resigned expression.

If only something would happen! It didn't matter what – even some misfortune! Anything but this suffocating calm.

She got up to go down to the stables.

Just then, one of the maids came in and handed her a telegram. She assumed it was for her husband. It was to do with business, no doubt. But it was for her. She opened it in great astonishment.

> YOUR FATHER ILL WITH PNEUMONIA. WISHES TO SEE
> YOU. COME IMMEDIATELY. RICHARD.

That was all. But it went round and round in her head.

If he were to die!

She had turned deathly pale.

'The telegram boy wants a receipt,' said the maid.

Selma wrote it out in a daze. Then she was left alone. The maid gave her a long, curious look before she went out.

But in that bewildered head there was one single thought: he was going to die. She had wished for some misfortune and now it was coming. God – who punishes those who do not believe – he had heard her prayer and granted it. This was his revenge.

She roused herself from her stunned state. She would have to leave at once. There was just time to catch the train.

For a moment she stood motionless, pressing her clasped hands to her face. Then she hurried down to order the carriage. It took five minutes to pack her trunk, and then all that remained was for her to write to her husband. She briefly informed him of the reason for her departure, enclosing the telegram in the letter.

Her arrangements complete, she set off.

The distance between her father's home and the station could be covered on foot in twenty minutes. She had never walked it so quickly, and it had never seemed so far.

When she reached the building, she rushed up the ramshackle wooden stairs and into the kitchen. There stood the old housekeeper at the stove, busy with something. Selma wanted to question her, but was too agitated and out of breath to utter a word.

The sight of her gave old Mätta a shock.

'Bless me, Madam, it isn't that bad,' she said, pulling off her kitchen apron, 'Calm yourself, dear Madam, it isn't that bad.' And she patted her consolingly on the shoulder.

Selma gave a sob.

'No, no,' protested Mätta, her own old face contorting, 'Don't cry, dearest Madam. I'll run in and tell Mr Richard.'

'No, I want to go myself.'

Selma passed through the succession of dilapidated rooms, with their tired rattle of dry, old doors. Her father lived at the other end of the building, where he had a separate entrance, but Selma had not dared to go in that way when she arrived, for she had a superstitious notion that she might find him lying dead.

In the drawing-room that adjoined her father's room, Richard was standing alone before the stove, in which a fire was blazing.

'Oh Richard, Richard,' said Selma, not even thinking to give him her hand, 'Do you think he's going to die?'

'No, I don't think so, but one can never be sure.'

Selma, shaking all over, pressed her handkerchief to her face.

'Come, come, take off your things,' said her cousin, coming over to help her remove her coat, which he hung up for her.

She threw her hat and gloves onto a chair and hurried towards the door.

'No, warm yourself a while first, it's raw outside,' he said.

'I can't wait.'

He stood in front of the door.

'You can't go in until you've calmed down,' he said crossly. There was nothing he detested more than tears.

She made no reply, but tried to get past.

97

'When you've calmed down,' he repeated, pushing her away.

'I *will* see him!' she burst out fiercely, trying to force her way in.

That made him angry.

'I've *told* you, that you may not!' he hissed in a half-whisper, took her by the arm and hurled her backwards with such force that she would have fallen if she had been less agile. As it was, she bent like a reed and absorbed the shock. When he removed his hand, she stood as tall and straight as ever.

She regarded him, suddenly calmer. His face was contorted with unreasoning rage, his face flushed, the veins on his forehead bulging. Then her expression brightened, and she gave a little smile, as if she had recognized an old friend, but did not wish to make herself known. She turned softly, still with that smile – went over to the sofa and paused for a moment with her back turned, pressing her handkerchief to her face. But she had stopped crying. Now it was pleasure she wished to conceal.

She was enjoying his brutality.

It was as if she had been given back what she had lost: all the years that had slipped by, her former self – everything!

She – the absolute ruler of her home – jaded, bored to death, she who could purchase for a caress anything that money can buy, who was obeyed by those around her for board and wages, stood there and enjoyed being told off like a dog; so great is the power of the new. But it was not only the novelty, it was also far more: it was also what had once been. It was the memories, the recollections – everything she had missed so bitterly – it was youth, life, freedom – all those things she had sold for money, all those things that are not directed and calculated, but come spontaneously. It was the freshness of testing another's will against her own, not with the compulsion to submit, but with the freedom to wrestle. She was neither the rich lady who must be obeyed because she paid nor the young woman who could demand because she could grant favours. She was simply the cousin, who must surrender or fight for her rights – just as it had once been.

She could have shouted for joy – and yet her father lay ill in there! But she felt safe now: Richard was here, wasn't he? Her own surly old Richard! She could have cried with happiness. There was no room for any other feeling.

He stood looking at her.

She was resting her left hand on the arm of the sofa, so her body was leaning a little and one shoulder raised. Her back was slightly arched, making the suppleness of her waist all the more striking, and the thick wool of her close-fitting, dark brown polonaise accentuated the firmness of her hips. Her figure had a purity of line that demanded attention.

The young doctor admired it too, but with purely professional interest. He thought about how strong and healthy that female form must be. And he compared it, without knowing why, with others he had seen, living and dead – which all merged in his mind into a single anaemic, tight-laced type.

'You're quite right,' she said calmly, turning round, 'I shan't go in to Papa until you say I may.'

This surrender was entirely voluntary; it was plain that it gave her satisfaction.

His look suddenly brightened, he came and sat beside her on the sofa.

'You can go in almost at once,' he said in altered tone, 'Let me just tell him you are here.'

She nodded her assent.

'I thought it my duty to inform you, although things are not too grave,' he said, 'And anyway, Uncle will feel comforted by your being here, and *that* will be as good as any medicine.'

'Of course you were right to inform me,' she replied. The tone of their exchange was as it had been in the old days.

And now they had an opportunity to look at one another while they chatted.

Richard looked like his father, but every feature was more pronounced, and things which his father could conceal with the caution of a clergyman were exposed to the light of day. There was something of the rebel in his appearance.

He was ugly, there were no two ways about it. That face could not be called winning in any way, but it gave a distinct impression of personality. Once seen, it could not be forgotten.

His forehead was wide; his brush of dark, curly hair cut short. His eyes were deep-set and too close together, giving a sharpness to his look; his nose was narrow and bold; his mouth broad, with thin, compressed lips. When he was not speaking, it was hidden by the beard and moustache – soft and curled – which covered the lower half of his face. It was a fine beard, and it suited him.

'Selma, I have something to tell you,' he said suddenly.

'What?'

He tried to keep his look neutral, but failed; he could not suppress a bright, sunny smile. His surly countenance had a remarkable capacity for transforming itself beyond recognition.

'I'm engaged,' he said, sounding a little embarrassed but keeping his eye fixed on her to see how she reacted.

'Oh, are you really – Dick – are you really?' she cried, pleased and surprised. 'Is it anyone I know?'

'No. But here's a picture.' He took a photograph from his wallet and gave it to her.

She studied it silently for a long time.

'Why were you so pleased?' he asked, trying to take back the picture.

'Don't, I haven't finished looking at it yet,' she said, elbowing his hand aside.

'So why were you so pleased, then?'

'Well, because if you're engaged, you'll presumably have to keep a check on your bad habits.'

He blushed crimson.

'Have I inflicted my bad habits on *you*?' he asked.

'Yes, always,' she replied with composure, 'But your fiancée should be able to teach you how to behave, she looks quite charming. Thank you!'

She handed back the picture.

'A beautiful blonde,' he said, looking at Selma's straggling fringe for comparison.

She flicked it out of her eyes with a toss of her head. It was a habit she had retained from girlhood. He noted it and had to suppress a smile.

'What's her name?' asked Selma.

'Elvira Kruse.'

'She's very young, I suppose?'

'The same age as you.'

'She looks younger in the photograph.'

'And in real life too, but that's because she's so small and slender.'

'Have you known her long?'

'For about as long as we've been engaged.'

'So you fell in love with her at first sight?'

'Yes, instantly,' he said with pride.

'How did it happen?'

He laughed.

'Well, what happened was that I was one of the groom's attendants at a wedding. She was a bridesmaid, and they drew lots, as so often in life, to pair us off. I got her. Now you know the whole story.'

'Shame on you!'

'Well, if you didn't like that I'd better try telling it another way,' he said with a smile. 'I and my comrades in misfortune walked into a room where the bridesmaids were standing waiting in a row. I saw fuzzy gold hair, as light as yours, but not so straight and heavy; it was as smooth as silk and wavy right down to the forehead, right down to the eyes, and it gave me a start when I saw it, and under that golden bird's nest I saw the sweetest little face, with such a soft, kissable mouth ... There, are you satisfied now?'

She sat looking down at her lap, laying one hand on top of the other and then drawing it away again, as if she were taking off gloves.

'Yes, but I don't like hearing you talk about it that way. Marriage is a serious matter.'

'But not quite as serious as going and hanging yourself. We all have to go some day, as the old woman said, when she chopped the head off the cock.'

She did not reply, nor did she look up.

'Do you want to see Uncle now?' he asked.

101

'Yes.'

'I'll go in and see how he is first,' he said, stood up and left the room.

Left alone, Selma leant back on the hard sofa and looked around the old room, where everything was so familiar. It had probably been lovely once. The large stove had a broad, decorative shelf apparently designed for ornaments, and that wallpaper with its design of landscapes, now ruined by damp and hanging off in large strips, had been costly in its time. It had all been inherited from the previous occupant.

Now there was hardly any furniture, and the pieces that there were did not go together. The room had been unused for as long as Selma could remember. She mentally rearranged the furniture as she sat waiting for her cousin.

He returned, and they went through the little lobby that lay between the sickroom and the drawing room.

Her father had a high fever and his breathing was laboured, but he did not look as bad as she had expected. She stood at his bedside and gently stroked his soft, grey hair.

Richard sat over by the desk and looked out into the courtyard, not wishing to intrude on their first meeting.

'Selma,' he said at last.

She went over to him.

He wanted to give her some instructions about the medicine.

She sat down on her father's desk chair, with the seat cover she had embroidered herself, and they spoke in low voices.

'We've prepared the guest room for you,' said Richard, 'because I was sure you would come.'

'Thank you. How did you find out that Papa was ill?'

'Mätta sent word with the man who brings the butter, so I came out here at once to see how things were, because the old fellow couldn't explain himself properly. I caught the midday train back into Lund to talk to the professor and get some medicine, and then came out here again.'

'That was very kind of you! But you'll stay here for the time being, won't you? It would be such a comfort.'

'Yes I will, that's why I brought some books with me. Last

night I sat up in that armchair, fully-dressed, but tonight you can take the watch.'

She nodded.

'That was my first time as a night nurse,' he said with a smile, 'I felt so sorry for old Mätta; she didn't sleep a wink the night before. But now I know why those nurses are so desperate for coffee. When Mätta came with the tray at about five, she seemed to me a truly angelic apparition.'

Selma gave a quiet laugh.

'And then I wanted a fire lit in the drawing room, so we could sit there to be near at hand,' he went on. 'But the stove was in a wretched state. I had to fill some of the cracks in the mortar myself – you should have seen me! – but now it's first-rate.'

And Selma thought she could see him; she knew his dogged eagerness so well, and she had to smile at his new-found skill.

'How very nice it is to see you at last!' she said.

He did not reply, but appeared to think the same.

'Where will you sleep?' she said.

'In the dining room.'

'Yes, that's excellent, then we can eat in the drawing room.'

'Very well.'

That made them laugh again: it was so funny making all these arrangements.

In spite of the worrying reason for her visit, this proved a wonderful time for Selma. She was in her best and calmest frame of mind, and since her father's illness took no turn for the worse, there was no cause for alarm.

The domestic staff consisted solely of old Mätta, ruling alone over kitchen and storeroom, and it was so quiet in the big house that the rats could be heard gnawing there in broad daylight. For Selma, there was something attractive about that desolate decay. She experienced the same delight as a rich man's children do when escaping from their expensive toys into a shed full of old junk, where it is up to them to make discoveries and retrieve things from the dust and oblivion. It was as if the very cobwebs in the corners, the tattered paper on the walls, lent the place a restful, carefree air.

'Isn't this a dear old owl's nest?' she would say to her cousin. And he would agree. There was something bohemian about it all which appealed to them both, because it was so unlike their normal, everyday lives. They felt somehow out of this world, and time seemed to stand still. They were both glad that their old intimacy had returned, unclouded by the arguments of before.

Every other day Selma would write to her husband, and she received letters at the same intervals – romantic love-letters with long quotations from poets like Vilhelmina and Tegnér. But there was one thing Selma never mentioned, and that was her cousin.

While the invalid was still at his worst, she and Richard took it in turns to sit with him at night, and whichever of them was not on duty would make early-morning coffee for the other. They always took it in the drawing-room, by the newly-lit fire, and this gave rise to much joking and laughter, because Richard was always so 'domesticated' and 'self-important' about it all, but something always went wrong; or so Selma said, and that gave rise to little, light-hearted disputes, logical evidence presented by him and little paradoxes thrown in by her. The way the coffee was served was anything but smart: thick, country crockery, tin spoons and a little, brightly polished coffee pot, which they privately referred to as 'Peter'. But the coffee was good and steaming hot, the fire sang quietly, and everything had that fresh, newly awakened feel. There was great camaraderie between them, and Selma said they were living like a couple of bachelors, but Richard laughed and said:

'Stuff and nonsense! As if you know anything about it.'

When he was not reading, they helped each other in the first few days to furnish the drawing-room with anything suitable they could find in the other rooms. They took great pleasure in it, trying and changing things over and over again and laughing at their own childishness, but finding it none the less enjoyable for that. They finally agreed that they had now made the drawing-room 'thoroughly elegant'. The truth was, at any rate, that they felt at home there, and that it now looked lived-in.

Richard wrote often to his fiancée.

One evening, when Selma came in from the sickroom, he

showed her three sheets of paper covered with writing.

'Look at the length of it,' he said, laughing, 'Now I've given her a picture of the owl's nest and of you as well.'

'Good gracious, what on earth can you have to say that can amount to such volumes?'

'Would you like to read it?'

'You surely wouldn't want me to?'

'Yes I would. Why not?'

'I didn't think anyone let other people see letters like that,' replied Selma, a little self-consciously. She felt offended by his offer, on his fiancée's behalf as well as on his.

'Well, you and Elvira are going to be friends, of course, and so you're most welcome to read the letter and add a greeting of your own. I've already mentioned that you're going to. I introduced you earlier in the letter. So it's all right.'

He was sitting at the desk, over in one corner, where the lamp was lit. All the blinds were down, and it was so warm and cosy in the great, gloomy room with its old-fashioned, rounded furniture, and the only light concentrated on his dark face, on his black, stubbly hair and broad shoulders.

He spread the letter out in front of him and looked at her; she approached, still seeming to hesitate.

'I'll bet you would as soon forego reading this as you would having food to eat, because women are always nosy, but they still act so damned prudish, that ... '

He stood up and slammed his writing-case down onto the desk with a crash.

Selma laughed at his outburst.

'Yes, that's just how it was the other day,' he went on, heated and unstoppable, 'when you happened to open that anatomy textbook. God preserve me! – you, young lady, a married woman, blushed and went pale at the same time and shut the book in alarm. Oh yes, I saw you, though I said nothing. And you were all ready to be annoyed that I was reading it. A doctor! – It would have been enough to make me laugh my head off, if I hadn't been angry enough to burst. What way is that to behave, making a fuss about a scientific textbook! And in any case, those are things that every woman should know about. If it had been anyone but *you*, I wouldn't have said a word. But as it is ... ugh, it's enough to make me sick! Are *you* going to go all affected, too? Just like Elvira.'

He broke off.

'How you do take on about nothing,' she remarked serenely.

'About nothing?' he repeated indignantly, holding out his hands in violent appeal, with a huge shrug. 'If it had been a tasteless novel, some immoral bit of smut, I wouldn't have said anything, but a purely scientific work...'

Selma merely gave a resounding, hearty laugh. She was so used to it all from earlier days that she almost enjoyed it.

'Well, how can humanity ever be improved, if women are going to persist in cocooning themselves so you can't even talk to them as human beings. The simplest things are improper. They positively beg to be considered idiots.'

Selma stood watching him with a calm little smile. She was simply waiting for the storm to subside. While it lasted, she knew there was no point in saying a word in any case.

'You may laugh,' he said more quietly, 'but this is serious. The next generation is totally dependent on you, on women. And where reforms are needed, in various areas, you could be our best allies. But – if you please – as soon as we venture beyond nice topics for the drawing room, you cover your ears and pretend to know nothing. You can't be taught to look after your bodies or your babies, because it is considered most improper even to name either of them. See, you're going red, just because I mentioned babies! – and you a married woman. Good grief, it's enough to make me ...'

He made a despairing gesture, as if he were trying to shake something off.

'Oh come on, Richard, what are you making such a fuss about! Have I ever refused to listen to what you've got to tell me?'

'Refused? Refused?' he echoed. 'Well, you've done your best! Look at you now, standing there squirming like an eel, as soon as you're invited to read a letter from me to my fiancée. As if there might be something in it to embarrass her ladyship; as if I can't be the judge of my obligations to Elvira.'

'You should be ashamed of yourself,' she cried gaily. 'Fancy blaming me for being tactful enough to have reservations.'

'But I don't want you to be tactful! There's nothing in the world I despise more than that.'

'Fie, what a hothead! I should walk out on you this minute, but now I feel like reading the letter, after all.'

'To do me a favour, to make me happy – no doubt! Huh, that's just like you. No thank you very much; I don't accept that kind of – charity.'

He gave a sneering, lopsided smile.

'But Richard!' Her tone was so disarming, it positively implored, and her smile had a sad look.

He did not answer, only resumed his seat in sullen silence.

'Well?' she said.

'There it is,' he indicated the letter. 'But it's all the same to me now.'

She said no more, but leant one arm on the desk and the other on his shoulder, bending forward to read. He was still surly, but she pretended not to notice. The pressure of her arm on his shoulder was steady and hard – disinterested, as if she were resting it on a dead thing. He saw it and was glad. That firm weight implied neither embarrassment nor pleasure. To her, he might as well have been a block of wood, and he sat thinking how ridiculous it was, that *that* could seem so agreeable.

He would have liked to say that it felt as though she were his sister, now – but it would have been a platitude, so he remained silent.

Selma pointed to the salutation in the letter. 'Dear Elvira,' it said.

'Is that what you always write?'

'Always. Why do you ask?'

'Just curious,' she answered, but blushed. She thought it sounded so simple and lovely. And the fact that he always put the same thing! Because those very words expressed the truth. The Squire was in the habit of finding endless variations: 'Dearest darling', or 'Adored wife', or 'My sweet love'. There was nothing to get a grip on, nothing real. And he would always sign himself 'Your beloved Paul'. It was ludicrous and irritating. Had she ever said that she loved him? That was a word she never used. Well actually, it was in the marriage vows. But then she had repeated it as soullessly as a parrot.

She turned to the end of the letter to compare. 'Your Richard,' it said. Nothing more.

He laughed, back in good humour again, and they read together, heads side by side. It was apparent that she was enjoying the letter.

'I had no idea you were such a master of style,' she said, turning a page.

'Well, I do need to apply myself; I'm going to be a writer, after all,' he replied.

'You!' She gave him a little nudge.

'Yes, in my specialist subject – of course. Once I've done my spell of duty at the hospital and all that, and then travelled abroad, I shall take up lecturing in popular medicine. There are all sorts of things I want to get the general public interested in.'

'Oh! That sounds fun; I shall read what you write. Do you think I'll be able to understand it?'

'Of course.'

She smiled with satisfaction; then she went on reading. The whole letter was about the old house, about herself – a very lively description – and about their life there. His style had an intensity that she found compelling. But not a word about love or anything like that.

'Hmm,' she said with a certain pleasure, when she had finished reading and straightened up again.

'Wasn't it to your taste?' He looked up at her a trifle mischievously, as if he had guessed her thoughts.

'Oh yes, it was extremely nice. But do you always write that way?'

'Which way?'

'So,' she sought the words, 'so – sensibly.'

They laughed; because it was so hard to express what she

meant, but so easy to understand it.

'Yes,' he said.

'Do you talk like that when you meet, too?'

His deep-set eyes flashed as he looked up.

'Do you think I'm that tame? Oh no, I can speak another language. But what's the point of using it in letters? No, a letter is a letter, and a kiss is a kiss. I let things be themselves.'

His words hit her like a dull pain she could not account for.

There was a pause. Selma leafed distractedly through some papers on the desk.

'Richard. You are really fond of your fiancée?' she said, in a very low voice and without looking at him.

'What do you mean by that?'

'I only mean, that it truly is a sin to ... ' She broke off.

'What's a sin?'

'Marrying a poor girl, and then letting her drift aimlessly, without taking any notice of her.' She spoke quickly and timidly.

He sat there, folding up his letter. There was something in her muted tone that suddenly caught his attention, pinching and pressing in on him – formless and uncontrollable, like a mountain dweller's longing for home, when memories are awoken. He would not have been able to look up just now for anything in the world.

'I am very fond of Elvira,' he said, 'I wouldn't want to lose her for anything. Selma, I'm so in love, that I'm quite wild at times. I'm jealous too. Can you imagine *that*?'

He spoke very softly. His tone contained something of the shame of confession, but also of the indignation in a complaint.

'I can believe it,' Selma replied.

Silence fell. He was still busy with his letter, and Selma seemed to be paying close attention to an old envelope.

'If any marriage *can* be happy, ours will be,' he said quickly, in a different tone. 'She's still so immature, so malleable and childish, I shall be able to educate her just as I wish. That means she will have to learn to understand me, and we will enjoy real fellowship.'

Selma said nothing; she ran her finger along the edge of the desk, deep in thought.

'But it's strange to think that she's the same age as you,' he added.

'Nineteen is no age at all,' answered Selma with a smile that concealed a hint of melancholy.

'No, that's true, but one always thinks of you as older.'

Chapter 7

Selma's father was improving with every passing day, and the Squire began to talk in his letters of coming to fetch her.

It was a misty spring day, mild and lachrymose, with great teardrops suspended from the eaves, and everything enveloped in a veil of moisture. Selma was sitting in the sickroom with her father, who was now well enough to sit up in bed and read the newspaper. He was newly shaven and his thin hair lay neatly combed on his shapely head. Selma had let her work fall into her lap and was resting her head on the high arm of the chair. She looked tired, and closed her eyes.

'You have been spending too much time at my bedside, child,' her father said in his thin, gentle voice, weakened by illness.

'You mustn't think that,' she answered with a smile, looking up, 'but I'm the sort of outdoor person who can't bear sitting still; I must have fresh air and exercise. Don't worry, my dear old Papa, when you're better I shall make up for it.'

He cast her a long, anxious look, and went back to his paper.

Selma closed her eyes again. She sat thinking about old times and what her uncle had done. Her lips formed into a hard, straight line, the taut mouth made her chin seem even sharper than usual, her brow knitted with a painful intensity and her whole face seemed contorted.

She now understood his motives. His own nature had led him to form an ideal of happiness, and that was what he had been trying to achieve for her. But had the intentions that prompted his actions been twice as good, she could still never forgive him. Never! And as if the damage he had done were not enough, he had been deceitful as well. She recalled a particular scene, when she had been in his room, asking to read a letter from her father, and he had refused. How foolish she had been to believe him! She had been so stupid throughout. It was because she was so honest. Was it foolish to be honest? Perhaps. But it was still hard to believe that what was right was foolish. And lying ... that must be wrong. – But she had ceased to communicate. She was never frank, not even with her father. She did not know how to be so any longer, not even with him. It was just an idyll, a pretty little childhood idyll that she cherished. Nothing more. – In fact she had always been uncommunicative on the subject of what she was thinking. She wondered whether her uncle knew that she ... well, she wouldn't quite say that she hated him, because that sounded so melodramatic, but even so, she bore him a grudge that could never be wiped away.

He would have acted in precisely the same way if she had been his daughter. What of it? Was she obliged to like him for it?

But it was fruitless to brood about herself, and most fruitless of all to grieve over the past.

She opened her eyes and looked about the room. She had to smile. It seemed to her that each piece of furniture was cursing the rest; the dark colours mumbling and the garish ones shrieking. Oh, how funny it looked! Yet Papa felt comfortable with it all! He didn't want to part with the tiniest item, and had constantly added new elements. She sat taking stock of everything.

The old pearl-coloured bed, which he would not be without for all the world, simply did not go with the modern basket-chair at the desk; the brown-stained armchair with its high back looked so grandfatherly beside the gaily-coloured bedside rug. But so much of it spoke of her, from her first awkward attempts at drawing, in frames salvaged from attics and lumber rooms, to the large photograph of her with its embossed mounting. From the doorpost hung her discarded skates, above the bed she could see a watch-holder, stitched by her at boarding school, and in one corner was the old wooden stool on which she used to sit as a child.

How wonderful it was to be alive! She smiled and shut her

eyes tight, rolling her head from side to side on the back of the chair to ease its aching.

The sparrows were making a terrible noise out there in the pile of brushwood in the courtyard. Apart from that, all was quiet. The watchdog came running out of its barrel, its chain dragging across the edge, and then stood on the barrel to shake itself, setting all the chain links rattling. She heard it all. And she realised that she was enjoying it. It didn't matter that her head was aching.

Then Richard came in.

She recognized his step and did not need to look up to know it was him.

'What's this! I do believe you're pretending to be ill, ma'am,' he said cheerily.

'Yes, just imagine! I've got a headache,' she replied happily.

'I can well believe it! It's no good for you of all people, this never getting out.'

'No, I know. And that's why I don't feel well. But I shall lie down for a while, then it will pass,' she said, getting to her feet.

'You can take a little nap on the drawing room sofa,' he said, and they left the sickroom together.

'I'll go and fetch you a blanket,' Richard said.

'Thank you.'

He came back almost at once, placed a pillow for her head and held the blanket ready.

She lay down.

'If you want to sleep, I'll go, otherwise I'll sit here with you and talk,' he said, arranging the blanket over her.

'No, sit here with me, I'm sure I won't get to sleep. Oh, that feels so nice!' she added, pressing her forehead to the cool pillow.

He brought a chair up to the head end of the sofa.

'Listen, Richard,' she said after a while, 'I've been thinking: you must have seen my mother when she was alive.'

'Yes, but I hardly remember her; I was only five when you were born.'

'I'd so much like to know something about her. I've never

113

been able to ask Papa; he just starts crying.'

'You know, my only memory of her is of lots of light hair and a big pair of hands that held me tight when I sat on her lap.'

She looked at him as though expecting to see something remarkable. He noticed, and a good-natured twinkle came into his eyes, but he said nothing.

'As I go around here, touching all the old furniture and things,' she went on, 'it makes me so curious. I feel like asking all these cupboards and drawers questions, and I go through everything I can find, just like an inquisitive child. Papa would never allow me to do it if he knew; it would make him quite ill.'

'And ... ?' he smiled.

'Well – it does me no good. Everything of Mama's looks so unfamiliar, as if it's all been dead and buried for years too. And I feel so empty – just as if I'd never had a mother.'

'Do you know what, people who haven't got a mother always imagine it to be such a wonderful thing, but it's not like that at all. It's just an acquired – hm – romantic notion.'

'Do you think so?' she said dubiously.

'Yes, I'm sure of it, in many cases. So-called blood ties are not at all as important as people claim. There are so many other things that are stronger. What more is there between Mama and me, for example, than that she spoilt me, so I found growing up more difficult than I otherwise need have? I can't talk to her about the things that really interest me, can I? She wouldn't understand.'

Selma looked thoughtful.

'However cold Papa may be, I feel more drawn to him,' he continued. 'Mama has had so little to do with my intellectual development.'

'That may be the case for boys,' she admitted, 'but not for girls.'

'You're not going around imagining yourself grieving for a mother you never saw? I would have thought better of you.'

A hint of derision flashed in his grey eyes, and she blushed furiously, knowing that he hated dreams and fancies of any kind.

'That's not what I mean,' she said in some confusion. 'I mean that a young girl, who had no female ... that is to say, no mother, doesn't turn out like other girls. I wasn't like the rest.'

'In what way?'

'I was so ... so ...'

She lay there without looking up, idly slapping one corner of the blanket against her hand.

'See, now you're being prudish again!' he said.

'No I'm not, I just can't find the right word. There, you see, it must be because I didn't have a mother that I'm shy and awkward like this.'

He burst out laughing. 'Now you really are being too naive!'

'Yes, I know, I always have been. That was my misfortune.'

He suddenly grew serious.

'Yes, you may be right about that,' he said, 'but it might have been the same, even if your mother had lived. Presumably you learnt a thing or two at the girls' school, anyway?'

'Me? No.'

'You must have done, from your friends. That's the usual way.'

'Oh no, not at *that* school,' said Selma with great spirit. 'You should just have seen Mrs Steel! I often think about her, now I'm older. She was separated from her husband, and ran the school so she could bring up her daughter herself. She never accepted girls above the age of nine, but those she took could stay as long as their parents wanted. She had a way of scaring all your thoughts away! She put us all in such dread of anything that could be considered improper, that even when two of us were chatting privately we dared not utter any word Mrs Steel would have condemned. She wasn't cruel, but we didn't like her. There was something oddly cold and unnatural in her manner, even towards her daughter. You always felt her big, brown eyes on you, even when she wasn't there. I've never seen such sharp eyes; you felt just like a pane of glass, and I know that if I ever had a thought ... some bit of innocent nonsense, love and that kind of thing, like girls usually do, I'd blush to the tips of my ears, even if I was quite alone, in fact even if it was pitch-dark.'

He did not answer immediately, but crossed one long leg over the other and clasped it, scrutinizing his boot as though it were something remarkable.

'How very strange,' he said finally, uncrossing his legs. 'I'd never have thought it.'

'No, I find it incredible myself. And you must bear in mind too, that Mrs Steel's school was in a village, out in the country; we weren't allowed to go any further than the garden, and we never met anybody. It was like living in a convent. So what could we be expected to know of the world and of human nature?'

'Hm. Papa thought it was an excellent school. That was why he wanted you to go there.'

'Well it was, in many respects. All I mean to say is that it made us unlike other people.'

'Maybe there was no harm in that, in a sense,' he said slowly. 'But it's not how I think children should be brought up, at any rate. What I detest most of all is the way women feel obliged to pretend ignorance of everything – that deplorable shamming every mother thinks she must teach her daughter, looking down and blushing at everything, or – even worse – blushing, giggling and turning away, if anyone happens to let slip a single word on subjects that ... that aren't at all a laughing matter. I get so furious, I could hit them.'

Selma could not restrain a smile.

'Well, don't you agree? Can't we talk sense and be serious with each other, even if one of us is a man and the other a woman?'

'Yes, of course.'

'I've told Elvira so many times, but no doubt it's her mother who's stuffed her with all that nonsense. Since we definitely will be married to each other one day, I do think I should be able to talk to her as I would to a really good friend. That's what she's promised to be, for our whole lives, so what kind of charade is it, making me sit and converse with her as if we were at a dinner party? There are so many really serious things I'd like us to exchange views on, but we can't. Like that, you can be together day in and day out and still not get to know each other. I'm supposed to be some sort of attentive admirer, nothing more. Is

116

that reasonable?'

Selma said nothing. She seemed to want to avoid being drawn on the question. He had been expecting her to take his side, and now he felt frustrated, disappointed.

'Richard, what does Uncle think of the match?' she asked suddenly.

'He says nothing; he knows there's no point. What I want, I want.'

'But you know what he thinks, of course?'

'Yes – that I ought to have married a rich girl instead.'

'Is Elvira poor?'

'Well she certainly hasn't got a fortune. Her mother has a pension or annuity, so they're well off. But Elvira is a much-fêted girl, and that costs money. I think we shall just about make ends meet.'

'Well, you were right not to think about money,' said Selma frankly.

Richard laughed.

'I agree, but even so, I'm quite sceptical about so-called love.'

He distorted the word, making it sound grotesque.

'You!? When you yourself are ... ,' Selma looked shocked.

'Yes. I am in love, yes,' he said drily, 'but I have been before, and it passed.'

'Yes, but you can't have felt then as you feel now?'

'Oh yes I did. The only difference is that I was more naive then, but also more obstinate; I fought against it, and yet ...'

She lay watching him with great interest, almost sympathy you might say, but when he fell silent, she did not ask.

'It was *you* I was in love with,' he said abruptly, without looking at her.

'Oh, what nonsense!' came the irritated outburst in reply; she had evidently expected something quite different.

'Come on now, don't take it as a declaration of love or anything,' he said crossly. 'I said it was all over long ago, so I see no reason why we shouldn't talk about it perfectly calmly. Can't we?'

'Yes, of course.'

'Didn't you know?'

'How could I have?'

'Oh – I just thought ...'

He broke off, and only continued after an interval, in an expressionless, staccato manner.

'It was that Easter. When I came back from Lund. Remember? We hadn't seen each other since the summer. You only came to us after Christmas. I thought you had completely changed."

'I was as ugly as sin.'

'You were. I don't understand myself how it happened. Well – actually I do. But it was incredible that it lasted so long. That summer, the whole time I was at home ... I was annoyed with myself for it.'

'I could tell that.'

'Hm. Don't you think I was sceptical even then? Even though I was only twenty-one?'

'Oh yes, I'm quite sure you were.'

'But it didn't help. You see, romantic ideas do cling so. We've absorbed them from a young age. We can't rationalise them away, and they keep coming back, a hundred times over. I've still got a few shreds left. They hang on like the very devil. Don't you see that the very fact that I'm sitting here talking to you has a romantic touch?'

'But that would mean that everything ...'

'Yes, you're right – most things, anyway. We've all had our heads turned. Everything's got to be called something other than what it is, be gilded and transformed. Everything's turned upside down.'

'Now you're seeing the dark side of things again,' she said gently.

'Seeing the dark side? No, I'm not. If you could only follow my line of thinking, you'd see I'm right. But of course, you don't want to.'

'Now, now, Doctor, be reasonable,' she said with a smile, placing her hand on his arm. 'Don't lose your temper, keep calm; I shall listen to everything you have to say.'

He was silent for a moment, evidently trying to heed her

118

appeal.

'I usually do keep calm these days,' he said. 'Why is it that I always get heated when I talk to you? It must be because you look ... that is, there's something so cold and so ... it's as if you could never ever lose your head, never be impetuous or anything like that. You're – well, I don't know what! – It's like talking to a gatepost, and straining my very hardest to extract some sign of life from it; I labour away, getting more and more exasperated. That must be it – the way you let me go on.'

She smiled again.

'And if there did happen to be life in the gatepost, what would you be wanting to say?'

'Yes, that's just it,' he persisted. 'You being so cool and calm, so unlike other women; it makes me think that I can discuss anything with you, and how interesting it could be to hear your views on lots of things, but then ...'

'Mm, what then?'

'Well, as soon as I start, there's something saying "don't come too close" – and it's so infuriating, because it's so unnecessary.'

'But Richard, how can you get so cross about nothing? It's simply never occurred to me that I might need to keep you at a distance.'

'No, it may well be unintentional, but it's there all the same, and it's hurtful. I wouldn't think about whether you were a boy or anything else, if it weren't for your tone. Like just now. There's something that comes into your voice, something timid, reserved. You speak quietly, formally, as if trying to keep the whole conversation down at freezing point – no, it's not that! – but there's something that isn't natural. You've got a strong, alto voice that can be brisk and clear, but then it goes sort of husky and hazy; that's the part I can't stand. It's telling me something like: "Be careful, you're talking to a woman". And it's the same with your look. You're usually one to look people straight in the face, but you look down, or to the side ... it's all got to be so cool and indifferent. – Oh, it's all so womanish! What's it supposed to achieve? In my eyes, you're simply a human being, no more and no less; so what's it all for?'

'But Richard. It's the very fact that you're so dreadfully violent and suspicious that makes me feel so timid.'

He leapt to his feet and took a turn about the room before answering.

She pressed one hand to her forehead; it was aching so.

'There, it's got worse,' he said nervously, 'and this time it's my fault.'

She laughed.

'Now then, do come and sit down.'

'Do you want a vinegar compress?'

'No, I don't. But I do want to put an end to this squabble, once and for all.'

He came back and threw himself onto the chair.

'Come on, Dick,' she said, taking one of his hands – a large, thin hand, its veins standing out from the firm bone structure. 'Now I know why your manner towards me has been so changed all this time, but now we're to be friends, aren't we, like we were before? You can have no idea how much your unfriendliness has hurt me. I've never had anyone but you and Papa, you know.'

He withdrew his hand without reply.

'That's all well and good,' he said at last, 'but everything has to be approached so delicately, and that's what I can't stand. It's just humbug. Why, for example, shouldn't I be able to tell you now that I was in love with you, without you adopting that strange tone? It's over now, so what on earth's wrong with talking about it?'

'Well if it doesn't embarrass you to talk about it yourself, then it doesn't embarrass me,' she said, with some vehemence.

He gave one of his abrupt, sarcastic laughs.

'And what do you think it was, for example, that so enraptured me? You yourself? Your soul, perhaps! No, it was your skin, because it looked as soft to the touch as a length of silky velvet, cool-hued yet warm, as temptingly creamy as a peeled banana. Your soul? Oh yes! No, it was your hair, because it was like no-one else's; not auburn, or golden yellow, or anything like that but – well, I don't know, but so artless, so unaffected, so – well, so no-one but I could find it beautiful, I thought. And that was just it: no-one but I. Who else would it occur to? A plait flapping against your back, and a fringe straggling in your face, so you were always tossing it out of your eyes. That could never be called beautiful, but it was as natural as an animal pelt – and I was in love.'

'Richard!'

'Yes – and your figure, so tall and rangy, so cold still and so supple; no-one had yet seen it grow to fullness, but it was clear that it would, and you were so thin, that it looked as though someone need only put their arm round you with a little force to make you fold across the middle like a sheet of paper.'

'But Richard!' She suddenly sat upright, as if intending to get up and go.

'Oh come on,' he said good-naturedly, 'that was the way you were *then*, and I'll never see you like *that* again. As you are now, I have no special feelings for you. You're just like any other woman. But in those days, there was something about you that was enough to drive one mad. It's gone now. Come on, lie down.'

'Eugh, you're simply unbearable,' she said with a sigh, lifting her feet up under the blanket again, and lying back onto the sofa.

'All I wanted to say was that love's like that. Don't give me all that about it being beautiful! Just veneer. Scrape it, and see what's really underneath.'

He took out a cigar and lit it placidly.

'Well it doesn't concern me,' said Selma rather hotly, 'because I've never been in love, thank God. But I understand you, all the same, and I think it's horrid – for Elvira's sake.'

'You could see from Axel Möller precisely where all those romantic notions lead,' he continued serenely, taking the cigar between his fingers. 'If he'd been like other people, one could simply have said, "Stop that drinking, you swine." But he thought himself a misunderstood genius, a bard, an artist. There was no order in his life, but he still managed to put a gloss on everything he did. If he was being lazy, he'd turn a languid look on you and say "*dolce far niente*"; if he was drinking, he'd lift his glass like a theatrical hero and say "*forget*"; if you told him straight out that he was a waster, you'd be informed that you didn't "*understand*" him. He didn't care that he drove me half out of my mind. And yet, he could've been a fine boy, if his head hadn't been completely turned by novels and vanity. I expect he even found something sublime in dying of drink, don't you?'

'But Richard, he didn't. You know he died of pneumonia.'

'Of course he did, but it would never have come to that, if he hadn't already been such a wreck.'

'Ah? I think it was quite sufficient that Jöns Ols' Marie wanted him.'

'Why? You can't deny he was unusually good-looking! He'd fallen into some very loose-living habits, but there are plenty of women who find men who make a show of their vices the most attractive. He thought that was all part of being a poet, and that was when it all began. And after all, as far as education goes, he was a bright spark compared to Jöns Ols' Marie.'

Selma did not answer.

'I suppose you know the old man's dead?' Richard went on.

'No, I hadn't heard.'

'Well he is. And do you know what happened to all his son's drawings?'

'No.'

'Sold at auction after the old man died. Old Mother Möller let everything go under the hammer; she didn't think there was anything worth keeping. The farming folk bought them by the basketload, and now I suppose they've got them on their walls like cheap coloured prints. I didn't hear a thing about it until afterwards, or I would have bought up the lot.'

Selma drummed her fingers hard on the wooden arm of the sofa.

'I've always detested Old Mother Möller,' she said gruffly.

They turned to other subjects. Their talk was of life in Lund, Richard's fellow students, the teachers at the academy, and anything else that occurred to them. Dusk came creeping over them with slow steps. It was like an old friend, welcome to listen in on the conversation. And no-one thought of lighting the lamp.

They chatted on cheerfully and intimately, Richard occasionally taking a long puff at his cigar, renewing its fiery glow.

Selma lay watching him with a pleasant sense of security. Now and then she turned the pillow to feel its cool side against her aching head.

In the darkness, the soft, concentrated outlines of his features were dimly visible. His teeth shone white whenever he smiled, and his eyes glinted occasionally. That was all she could make out.

He was in good spirits, exhilarated even, for on the rare occasions when his taciturnity thawed, it was replaced by a jovial flow of words as unchecked as the most babbling brook of spring. Everyone was fair game. His comments ranged over everything and everybody, with a direct, coarse humour that was irresistible in its effect. Selma was laughing out loud.

Just then, the door to the other rooms opened, and the Squire entered.

Selma instantly knew who it was. She jumped up and threw the blanket on the sofa.

'Is it really *you*?' she said. 'Come on in!'

The Squire, coming from outside, could not see clearly. He moved towards her, and gave a start on seeing Richard. As for Selma – who was never ashamed of kissing her father, even if the whole world was watching – she felt shame would prostrate her as she offered two cold, indifferent lips to her husband. Involuntarily, Richard's words ran through her mind: 'Don't you think I can speak another language?'

How scornfully he must be smiling inside at this charade! ... must be comparing her with Elvira ... who was *his* because ... because ...

The Squire bowed stiffly to the young man, but did not proffer his hand.

'Don't you recognize Richard?' asked Selma in a strained voice.

'Why yes, of course,' replied the Squire with suppressed indignation in his voice. 'This gloom is ideal for recognizing people.'

It was meant to be sarcasm.

Selma went over to the desk and lit the lamp. She was neither sorry nor afraid, even though she could see the Squire was furious, but the thought that she would now be going back to her old life oppressed her.

There was an awkward silence. Richard and the Squire were like two dogs, circling one another at a stiff-legged strut, hackles raised, as they exchanged wary looks. It would have made Selma laugh if she had not been thinking of the journey home.

She took her husband in to see the convalescing patient; Richard stayed where he was.

'That was all very familiar, I must say, lying there in the gloom allowing yourself to be engaged in conversation by such a – cocky fellow. With *him* you could laugh, all right! He must be mightily interesting,' said the Squire in the little lobby.

'You forget that we grew up together,' she answered sharply, opening the door to her father's room.

'Well that could always be used as – a cover,' he mumbled.

Selma made no reply.

A little while after, Richard came in and handed her a short note from Elvira, which had been enclosed in his letter.

But he withdrew at once.

'So, you share your correspondence as well?' said the Squire, who had noticed that the letter had been opened.

'It's just a few lines from Richard's fiancée. But since you're so interested, you can read it first; I'm in no hurry at all,' said Selma, holding out the letter with a smile of anger.

'No, upon my word, that wasn't what I meant,' said the Squire apologetically, pushing back her hand. 'You read your letter. That wasn't at all what I meant. – So, he's engaged, eh?'

Selma read her note in silence.

The Squire paced to and fro across the floor with a thoughtful expression. He cast an occasional furtive glance at Selma, who sat there looking angry.

Several times he tried to draw her into the conversation he was having with her father; but she answered curtly, with the sort of cool politeness that was the most extreme expression of hostility she ever allowed herself.

The Squire was squirming in agony, not only at her displeasure, but also at his sense of having done her an injustice: the young man was engaged, after all!

'Listen, is it wise for us to stay so long here with father-in-law? Perhaps we should go into the other room for a while,' said the Squire at last, after a prolonged silence.

He very much liked saying 'father-in-law'; it was as if he himself became several years younger.

'Yes, let's go,' said Selma listlessly, 'I expect Mätta has the evening meal ready.'

So they went into the drawing room. Richard was sitting there at the desk, reading. The Squire went straight over to him.

'I hear from my wife that you are engaged, Mr Berg,' he said in his most gentlemanlike tone, while the young doctor regarded his benevolent expression with utter astonishment. 'I cannot congratulate you warmly enough on such a step; taking a liking to someone early in life is the best way for a young man to be preserved from temptation. I sincerely congratulate you. Is there any prospect ... I mean, in the not too distant future ... um ... When are you planning to get married, Mr Berg?'

'At the earliest opportunity – the very earliest opportunity,' replied Richard curtly. He was indignant at this unexpected interest in the affairs of his heart, after the previous hostility. Moreover, he considered the subject none of the Squire's business.

'Quite right, no long engagements,' affirmed the latter. 'They are nothing but a seething ebb and flow. I truly admire you for your sound views, Mr Berg.'

Richard thought to himself that he had not given his views at all, but he did not bother to say anything. He had always felt a certain animosity towards Squire Kristerson.

Suppertime was more bearable than Selma had dared hope after their first encounter. The Squire did not allow himself to be rebuffed by Richard's reserved manner, but maintained a sunny mood, and his attentiveness to Selma knew no bounds. At times it even made her laugh.

'Yes, respect for the fair sex,' declaimed the Squire with

125

pathos. 'Women rule the world.'

When they were leaving the next morning, he would not on any account allow Selma to walk to the station, although she declared loudly that she would prefer it.

No, she must be driven! And the Squire himself went in to see the leaseholder to arrange for a carriage. He supervised the harnessing of the horses, organized the luggage and everything. He also managed in passing to exchange a few words with Richard, and finally succeeded in arousing his curiosity.

'Selma,' Richard asked her as she happened to pass through the drawing-room, 'what in the world did you say to your husband yesterday evening to make him so favourably disposed towards me? When he arrived, he wouldn't even give me a civil greeting. I really didn't think you could be so sly.'

'Oh Richard, it was quite unconsciously done,' replied Selma, suppressing a smile. 'I just happened to tell him that you were engaged.'

He looked at her quizzically for a moment. But then he understood, gave a dry laugh and returned to his book.

A little later, they were both in the bedroom, where her father was up for the first time, sitting fully dressed in his big grandfather chair, downcast because his daughter was to leave him.

Richard and Selma stood by the window. She looked the picture of vigour in her close-fitting spring costume and jaunty deerstalker.

Through the window, the Squire could be seen attending to the carriage.

'Paul has given me leave to make some improvements to our farm labourers' cottages, the worst of them – of course,' she said hurriedly, adjusting her hat and securing it with a pin. 'And I so much wanted to ask your advice about various things, so I could do a good job and make sure they were healthy places to live; their blessed children are quite worn down with skin rashes and other wretched infections. Paul says children like that always are, but I can't reconcile myself to it. Every time I go there ...'

'Yes, what do you think you can do?' he said crossly, but a

twitching beneath his beard hinted at a teasing smile.

'But when they're *ill*!' ... Blushing, she gave him a reproachful look.

'My God, just like in the old days!' he exclaimed with a laugh. 'I recognize that expression so well. Go on then. I only wanted to hear what you would say.'

'Hm, I've been wanting to talk to you about it the whole time, but I've been sort of afraid.'

'Afraid? Of me? Why?'

'I thought you might laugh at me.'

She kept tugging at her glove, although its fit was already flawless.

'Laugh? It's my own pet subject, so why would I laugh?'

'We-ell,' she said slowly, 'I'm undoubtedly very ignorant; I don't know anything.'

'That's precisely why you need me.'

She appeared relieved at his answer.

'Well I think that since I've got easy access to money, I can ... Well there were lots of things I wanted to tell you, but now there isn't time.'

'Then write.'

She looked at him, pleased and surprised.

'Would you like me to?'

'Naturally.'

'Oh thank you, thank you!' she cried, overjoyed.

He just smiled.

'You can't imagine ... oh, you just can't imagine how time hangs heavy on my hands sometimes.'

'But what about your old passion for painting – is that all over?'

'Yes. Since I couldn't study it, or devote myself fully to it, there was no point. But it does feel empty.'

'Don't you ever intend taking it up again?'

'No, never.'

She glanced out into the courtyard and saw that everything was now ready.

'Goodbye then, you dear old thing,' she said, going over to the armchair and stroking her father's hair, which she herself had so neatly combed. She bent down and brushed her cheek against it. 'Now you must hurry and get well, and then you can come for a long, long visit.'

He said nothing, just squeezed her hand.

'Now you mustn't be sad!' She bent down and looked him so merrily straight in the eyes that his face brightened. 'You can come and see how well my riding is coming on. Goodbye then, dear, silly old Papa!'

She ruffled up his hair by way of farewell, which made him look very content.

'Goodbye Dick,' she said, turning to her cousin, who had been standing watching the two of them with a smile. 'I can't tell you what fun it's been to see you again, old fellow. And you'll come soon with Elvira?'

They parted with a firm handshake, and she ran out to the carriage.

Chapter 8

Selma was riding at a walk, and the regular rhythm of her horse's hooves rang out beneath the yellowing canopy of the park. The morning was cold, but the long ride had given her cheeks their warm colour.

Black Prince nodded his handsome head in satisfaction and gave the occasional snort, dipping his neck and flaring his nostrils to exhale swirls of steam.

Selma was twenty-three, but might be said to look older. Her deportment had grown more deliberate, her look more composed, and there was self-assurance even in the way she sat on horseback.

As she rode out onto the open garden walk that constituted the approach to the main house, the pair were suddenly in full light; her flushed cheeks glowed and the horse's coat glistened in the sun. The coarse gravel crunched beneath the horse's hooves and she cast a glance up at the windows to see whether anyone had noticed her arrival. At one of them she caught sight of a blonde female head and a white peignoir.

The groom who was riding behind her came forward to take her reins.

She dismounted lightly without assistance, took a look at her mount too check he was not too sweaty, and stroked his neck caressingly beneath the long mane. He turned to nuzzle her dress, rubbing his neck against her shoulder as he did so, leaving great, white flecks of foam.

'Oh, you naughty rascal!' she said, laughing, and wiped her dress with her handkerchief. She tossed the reins to the monstrous picture of ugliness who served as her groom, and went into the house, leaving Black Prince to watch her with his great, melancholy eyes. He apparently thought she was taking too long inside, for he lifted one hoof to paw the ground, but pawed only air. Prince was of a tactful disposition.

'Well, look at you! Are you really so impatient, you silly old thing?' she called down to him, coming out onto the steps with a huge slice of coarse rye bread in her hand.

Prince dropped his muzzle and gave a little shivering sound, meant to be the merest hint of an affectionate little whinny.

'Oh, you really are a perfect horse!' she exclaimed with pride, running down to feed him. She had removed her gloves to avoid getting them wet, for she knew from experience that Prince showed no consideration where bread was concerned. She stood bare-headed in the sunshine, watching in delight as her favourite contentedly munched on his bits of bread and rooted around in her hands with his muzzle, without the slightest inhibition. She had to stand well back and stretch her hands out to him, since he was displaying such a tremendous urge to rub himself against her dress.

'Now it's all gone,' she said gaily, holding up her wet hands so he could see it was true. He sighed with an air of resignation, and she drew his head to her, to kiss him on a nice, dry little spot on the side of his muzzle.

'There, there,' she said in conclusion, then wiped her hands and went up to the guest rooms, while Prince was led away to the stables.

'Well, Elvira, aren't you ready yet?' she called from outside the door.

'Richard went out more than an hour ago, do come in,' came the answer from inside.

Selma opened the door and went in. The elegant little pair of rooms was currently occupied by Dr Berg and his young wife, during their extended stay as Squire Kristerson's guests.

Mrs Berg was sitting at the mirror combing her hair. She was small and blonde, good-looking and with a tendency to plumpness.

'How can you bear not to open some windows, when it's such

lovely weather?' said Selma, as she closed the door behind her and nodded in greeting.

'Brr, it's so cold,' replied Mrs Berg with a little shudder.

'You indoor creature! What have you done with your husband?'

'Out for a long walk. He got annoyed last night because you said you didn't want him to come out riding with you today, and when he's cross about something, he can trudge for miles at a time.'

'Can he really still be cross today about what I said yesterday?' remarked Selma in a tone of indifference.

'Oh, you know how he broods on things.'

'He used not to be like that; I could goad him every day, and he was always back in a good mood by the next morning.'

Selma threw herself onto the sofa and contemplated with pleasure the waves of pale hair flowing through the comb over by the mirror.

'Do you know! – It's awfully nice looking at women – *nota bene*: beautiful women,' she exclaimed cheerfully, tapping the toe of her shoe with her riding crop.

'What a silly thing to say; you're a woman yourself!'

Selma gave a laugh.

'Yes, I certainly am, but there's none of that softness about me – the sort of thing that makes one feel you women can be wound round one's little finger.'

'I think you should have been a man; it would have suited you so well,' said Elvira, putting up her hair and leaning forward to the mirror.

'Yes, it would have been more agreeable, but I suppose things could be worse. I make quite a passable woman too: we don't all have to be identical. But look at me a minute!'

Selma strode over and put her arm round the young woman's shoulders, leaning forward to look into her face.

'I thought so! You've been crying again. What is it?'

'Oh, don't concern yourself.'

Selma paced the room.

'It's no good keeping it in all the time; tell me,' she said, coming to a halt beside the dressing table, where she could see the young woman's face.

'Oh, it's nothing at all ... it's only Richard ...'

'What about him?'

'You've already noticed.' Elvira rearranged her toilet articles, but she was clearly not concentrating on what she was doing.

'What have I noticed?'

'That he doesn't care about me.' Her head was lowered and she spoke very softly.

Selma stood looking at her with a peculiar look in her eyes that combined interest and distaste. Such prettiness could not fail to appeal to her appreciation of beauty, but anything effeminate filled her with disgust.

'Can't you tell me about it?' she said, looking down at the tip of her riding crop.

Elvira threw her a hasty glance. There was something initially repellent but ultimately winning about that mixture of bluntness and utter self-control. In her black riding habit, with its tight-fitting bodice and arms, she looked even taller than usual. Her hair was lifted high off her neck, but fell low over her forehead in a thick, light brown fringe, so that only a narrow strip could be seen above the rather darker eyebrows. In actual fact she was rather ugly, that flattened nose with its pointed tip, and that broad, low brow and fine, sharp chin, making her face triangular. But the wise, deep-set eyes made up for everything; she looked splendid.

'Although I'm no older than you, I've been married longer, so I've gained some experience,' said Selma, overcoming her distaste for speaking on the subject. 'Perhaps I can give you some advice that could help.'

'You're so good and kind,' said Elvira, keeping her at a distance with one of those phrases that women always have ready for each other.

'Kind! Wherever did you get such an idea?'

Selma looked almost angry.

'You're so good to everyone here on the estate; old Boel's told me your secret.'

'Old Boel should mind her tongue.'

'You're good to all the poor people on the estate.'

'Good! Do you call that good? I'm an egotist. It's only my need to feel useful to others that makes me do it; it's self-importance, nothing more. You can rest assured I only give away what I don't need or want myself. Is that being good?'

She said the words vehemently in her desire to convince. At the heart of her rather outspoken nature there was a reserve that made her inner being shrink from every touch.

'Now you're exaggerating,' said Elvira.

'Oh, don't make me sick! I give them food and money the same way people throw bones to dogs; their grasping greed disgusts me too, and if it weren't for the fact that I need to bask in their short-lived gratitude, I'd be just as happy sending them packing with a good kick. I don't know who's the vilest, them or me.'

They were words that concealed loneliness and suffering, but Elvira noticed none of it; she merely felt repelled by the brutality of the statement. She had no idea that there are people who are such fanatical lovers of the truth that they tell lies about themselves.

Selma threw herself back onto the sofa and passed her hand across her brow as she leaned back with a weary expression.

'I can't live without kindness,' she said, 'So I buy it ... that's the whole story. For money you can have everything, everything!'

'Not everything; not love,' replied Elvira emotionally.

Selma gave a short laugh, but said nothing. A look of scorn played around her mouth. She did not raise her eyes.

'Still, it is strange to see how our predispositions are laid down in us from the very start,' she said after a time, while Elvira paced the room. 'I remember, when I was at my aunt and uncle's out in the world – Richard's home, you know – I always used to hide away my cakes and biscuits when we had coffee, saying I needed them for "night starvation", as we used to say at school. Aunt used to laugh at my childishness, but she let me have my cakes. I would save them every day for a whole week. Can you guess what I did with them?'

'No.'

'Well, I'd come across a real old hovel out by the cattle shed. An old couple lived there with a whole brood of children around them. They'd already raised a brood each, because they'd both been married before – but I've never seen children like them. Dirty and ... oh, you can just imagine! So naturally, it was those little beasts my cakes were for. The parents were hardly ever in; the offspring had to fend for themselves like tadpoles. And believe me, they were so delighted, whenever I came! ... I sometimes tried to tell them stories, but they didn't understand them; I think I tried to teach them a little geography too, but that was no better. And I – who loved cakes myself – would sit there watching them devour Aunt's wonderful buns, licking my lips.' She laughed until the tears came into her eyes.

'Not that I suppose they could have tasted any particular difference between them and those doughy objects our village baker thought worthy of the name buns! And what's more, I imagined I was doing the children a good turn. I took pleasure in it, of course. And do you know, to crown it all, I decided I was going to comb their hair. But luckily I never put that into practice.'

It was apparent that she was very pleased with her dramatic account.

'Ooh, why do you always have to scoff at everything!'

'Just to see the funny side. I'm simply not one for tragedy.'

'I envy you that. After all, that must be what makes you so attractive.'

'Attractive? Ten to one you learnt that word from a novel!'

'Oh, you're horrid.'

'I've never claimed otherwise; you're the one who was trying to convince me of the opposite.'

Selma laughed, and Elvira turned away to hide the tears that were welling up in her eyes.

'Elvira!'

'Yes, you're like Richard, you think you can laugh everything off where I'm concerned.'

'You weren't concerned, I was. What's more, you're the one

who didn't want to say why you were upset, so I thought it best to talk about something else.'

Elvira sat down at the dressing table and put her head in her hands.

'Richard isn't himself, not like he was for the first year; there's all the difference in the world. You wouldn't believe how happy we were! He gave up all his friends, and we weren't parted for a single day. But since the little one arrived, he's been quite different. I sometimes think he doesn't like *him*. That's why I left the little angel with my mother when we came here. I thought it would make things better. But when does he talk to me, eh? He's kind and considerate – naturally – but we never have anything to say to each other, when we're on our own.'

'But my dear child, he can't always be talking, you know.'

'But when we were first married, he had a thousand things to talk about, and during our engagement.'

'I can well believe it! They always do have – a lot of nonsense which you'd get utterly sick of in the long run. You wouldn't want him to carry on like that?'

'Well, maybe not. But when I try to read in his eyes what it is he wants, when I do everything I can – big or small – to accommodate him! When all I think of in whatever I do is whether he will like it!'

'That's just the problem. You're doing too much for him, and he finds it wearisome. If only you showed a touch of independence.'

'That's just it! But it's absurd. Surely the people we like best are those who do as we want?'

'I'm not so sure; I think every human being was created to be an individual in his or her own right. If we try to make ourselves into mere copies, we're punished by becoming nothing.'

'He likes you for your independence, I know.'

'With us two it's something quite different, our relationship isn't a close one. But we have so many interests in common, old memories too ... and besides ... oh well, those are things I don't understand.'

'What?'

'Well, I think that in the long term a man will only care for someone who can keep him at a distance.'

She gave an ironic little smile.

'But a wife can never do *that*,' cried Elvira, turning round, almost in fright.

Selma was reclining on the sofa; she regarded her guest with a long, searching look, not without a hint of mockery.

'He knows that,' she said softly, still with that smile.

'What do you mean?'

'I mean it would be very easy to make a man fall in love again – it that's what you're thinking of. We don't know them before we marry them, but then we have to learn. I think *I'm* learning now.'

'I admit that I don't understand Richard,' said Elvira coldly, heating the stylus over the lamp to curl her fringe. There was something in Selma's tone that she did not like.

'Well study him then, it's high time. Learn to understand him – I mean all his ambitions and interests – you'll find that you enjoy it, and you'll learn so much from trying to keep up. But above all, try to be a little cold ... just a very little, as one can be when one is really fond of someone.'

She put her head on one side and prodded at the carpet with the tip of her riding crop. There was something restrained about her now, simultaneously gentle and mischievous, perhaps slightly sad as well.

'Cold?' echoed Elvira, utterly astonished.

'Yes, cold.' Selma spoke unusually quietly and without looking up, that mysterious smile still lingering around her thin, delicate lips. 'Love is like champagne – don't you know how it tastes when it's been on ice?'

'But Selma!' A tone of reproach came into her voice.

Selma jumped up with a merry little laugh, went over to Elvira and put her hands on her shoulders. Her previous harshness was gone.

'Now I'm your father confessor,' she said soothingly, 'Answer me honestly, my child. Do you sometimes cry and ask your husband to be as fond of you as he was before?'

'Yes.'

'Very occasionally?'

Selma had shifted her hands to the back of the chair, and the confessant drew imaginary figures on the dressing-table with a charming forefinger. But she said nothing.

'So you often do it?' continued the stern confessor, turning her head to make sure her ear caught the reply.

The confessant looked up, wondering whether she might dare to reveal the truth. Her expression was so comical that the confessor, despite her efforts, could not help bursting out laughing.

'Holy innocent! And you think that's the way to catch a man? Ah well, you are in love with him yourself, and that's just as well for *you*. On one hand it makes things harder, but on the other it makes them immensely easy.' She bent down so her face was on a level with Elvira's and looked at her in the mirror. 'Now, if that face looked happy and lively, it would be really enchanting, but when it's blubbing – ugh!'

Elvira looked in the mirror too.

When Selma smiled like that, so her even, white teeth glinted, there was no more invigorating sight to be seen. It was impossible to find her ugly any longer – even for a woman.

The little doctor's wife leant back and put her arms around her confessor's neck, but Selma laughingly freed herself: not all confessors want to be caressed.

Selma stood silent for a moment. It seemed to her that she held the key to his character in her hand, and everything she had hunted out with her sharp, perceptive eyes – everything she had loved best, because it had been hers alone, everything she had wanted to keep hidden as her most priceless property – she was now to place in another person's hands. Everything, everything! For there could be no compromise.

'Elvira,' she said, her voice sounding so serious, her words forming slowly, 'sometimes you find him irritable and restless. It vexes you. But have you never thought that it could be a moment of weakness, when everything seems futile and dark to him? Have you never thought that that's when he needs you most? ...

Not your words or your comfort, just quiet, and the feeling that you understand him. He has to feel that you will never lose heart, because you believe the best of him, even if he's doubting himself.'

Elvira rested her head in her hands and said nothing. Something akin to self-reproach flashed through her mind – a suspicion that she was still not loving as fully as she could. Slowly, she nodded to herself.

'So that's agreed,' said Selma briskly, suppressing the pang of pain which accompanied the very thought that her efforts might succeed, 'No tears, no more scenes; and I also think you should put aside your confounded Persian embroidery sometimes. There are surely other things in the world worthy of a woman's attention? Aren't you at all interested in our own time and where all its endeavours are leading? Child, eventually you'll have to learn to understand your own son! How can you do that, if you deliberately remain ignorant of everything and are only engrossed in your basket of Berlin wool?'

She stopped for a moment.

'Elvira, it must be a great joy to have a son,' she said suddenly.

'You!' said Elvira quickly, turning round, 'Do *you* ever think of such things? Do you really wish you had a child?'

'*I*? Good gracious, no! That wasn't what I meant. It was only a general statement. Take you, for example, who are so fond of Richard, I suppose it must be wonderful for you to think that his personality will be inherited in some way, that everything you value in him will grow up again, and feature after feature will emerge. I can just imagine what a joy it would be to discover each new likeness. There are even some faults one can learn to like, and I suppose that even if you chastise him for them, you still couldn't help being a little pleased if they were the same as well.' She stood looking out into the garden with a strange, self-absorbed look in her eyes.

Elvira had grown thoughtful.

'Selma, haven't you ever ... haven't you ever loved anyone?'

Selma awoke at the question.

'I! How could you think so?'

Both fell silent for a time, as Elvira looked in the mirror and applied a dash of powder to her fringe to stop it losing its curl.

'I think you could have been an excellent wife,' she said finally.

'Oh, that depends,' replied Selma listlessly, 'If I'd married a man with ambition, I would probably have been a great help to him – I would have urged him on, worked for him, but now,' - she made a gesture as if letting something drop through her hands - 'now I'm completely worthless.'

'Oh no, don't say that.'

'Well it's true, I keep the servants in line and make sure everything runs like clockwork, but anyone could do that as well as I do. You said a little while ago that I ought to have been a man. But you see, in me there's such a craving somehow to submerge myself in another's existence, which proves that I was really meant to be a woman. A man never feels that way.'

'Poor Selma!'

'Are you mad? Why feel sorry for me?'

'Well, because you've never experienced what it means to be happy.'

Selma laughed.

'That's what all young wives say. They think that there's no other happiness in the world but their own, and – with all due respect – I have my own views on that. I feel no envy whatsoever. If it weren't for my being such a miserable coward that I can't bear to see anyone sad, I'd never have interfered in your affairs, my dear.'

'I believe you do truly wish me well.' Elvira held out her hand, which she took, fleetingly.

'Of course I would very much like to see you happy,' she said brusquely, 'And preferably to see that you both had me to thank for it in some way or other. It's just like when I gave those children my ginger biscuits' – she gave a bitter, self-deprecating laugh – 'So let me choose books for you and supervise your studies; I know Richard's taste so well. If you put your mind to it, you can become a completely new person while he's off on his tour abroad. But don't ever show him my letters, or let him venture to open them; you have to make him respect you in these matters. And if you let him fly the nest freely, he'll be all the happier when he comes back.'

'You may be right.'

'Of course I am! You've no idea how keen I am to try out my cure on someone,' she said jokingly. 'Unfortunately I've no need of it myself.'

'You know, I've grown awfully fond of you while I've been here,' exclaimed Elvira.

'Oh, but there's a kind of egoism that's very attractive,' came the merry retort. 'Mine is just that kind. People can't *help* liking me if I want them to. There's only one exception to that rule; I'm quite powerless against him, because ... well ... Not a word more. You'll never finish dressing at this rate.'

'Oh yes, that reminds me, please excuse me from breakfast today; I ate so much with my coffee earlier that I'm not hungry, and I must write to Mama now, otherwise the letter won't catch the post, and then Mama will worry.'

'As you wish.'

Selma nodded and left the room.

At first she intended changing her dress, but she thought better of it: it was so unpleasant going into the bedroom, where her husband still lay sleeping and the beds were unmade. She preferred to wait. She went instead to the little chamber that led off the drawing room. It always afforded silence and solitude, and there was a view over the park. She stood by one of the windows, absorbed in thought.

It was eight-thirty. Where had Richard got to? Perhaps he had lost his temper in earnest? She could not believe it. He ought to have understood her motives. Surely he knew ...?

She leant her forehead against the window frame and put one knee up on the sill, as if riding side-saddle.

What a peculiar disposition he had! In his student days there had only been vague hints of it, and she – a child herself – had not really understood them. It manifested itself more decidedly in the young doctor and scientist, and she was also a mature woman now.

There was something fundamental to his character that inevitably resonated with her own. Firstly that well-developed willpower, which turned into ruthless egoism whenever a goal was in view; then that dogged endurance, which never let the goal slip from sight; and finally that ambition, which constantly spurred him on and never gave him any rest. But she also knew that there were moments when his highly-strung self-confidence deserted him, leaving him so dispirited that he felt too numb even to work. In the depths of that intractable mind ran an undercurrent of which he was ashamed, and which he tried to hide beneath cynicism or severity. Perhaps it was that undercurrent which drew her to him.

Selma slid down from her place and returned to her lookout post. He must come soon. How deathly empty it would be when they left! She folded her arms and stared gloomily ahead. What an existence!

From where she stood in the little chamber, the whole apartment spread before her, with its rich draperies and soft carpets – carpets covering the whole floor and creeping from room to room, stretching away in the same, interminable pattern. It was an elegant little corner room, papered pale grey with a design of brightly coloured little nosegays – everything was soft, cushioned, comfortable.

The dark female form stood out like a silhouette against this light backdrop, and the luxurious comfort of the room lent greater emphasis to the unadorned simplicity of her riding habit.

Selma was so absorbed in her brooding that the doctor was able to come right into the drawing room without her noticing. He drew aside the curtain and walked quietly up to her. Only when he put his hand on her shoulder did she turn round, calmly and without giving a start: this experienced horsewoman did not know the meaning of the word nervous.

'What are you standing there thinking about?' he asked, now beside her.

'All manner of things. You and me and old times.'

'Isn't your husband up yet?'

'No. He didn't get home from the grand opening of the

railway until three this morning, so he needs to sleep.'

'Then what harm would it have done him if I'd come out riding with you?'

The question was put bluntly and a little provocatively.

'Not the slightest, of course. Nor was it for his sake that I said no, but for my own.'

'So you didn't *want* my company, thank you very much! At least you gave me a straight answer. Yesterday I thought you had another reason ... which I admit I considered a bit cowardly, but ... '

He did not mean what he was saying, but had almost convinced himself that he did. The desire to sound her out was not entirely conscious.

'Oh Richard, now you really are being silly,' exclaimed Selma with something of her old tone, putting her hand on his arm to emphasize her point. 'I'd be very glad of your company, you should realize that. Just imagine how delightful it would be to have you at my side to talk to as we rode slowly along. I can sometimes imagine it so vividly that I almost feel you're there and we're discussing all sorts of things.'

He looked at her, his face clearing, and she quickly withdrew her hand.

'Well, you know, I think it must be so easy conversing as you're gently rocked, the way you are on horseback, to the soothing sound of clip-clopping hooves. How lovely it is! You can feel the warmth of the horse's body right down to your feet, and the cold, fresh air around you ... Ugh, how childish you must think me!'

She threw her riding crop onto a table and clasped her hands together, stretching out her arms with a hint of defiant spirit. She made such a beautiful figure, her arms slender yet strong.

'Then I don't understand ...'

'Oh yes you do. Kristerson doesn't bother to be jealous of you now you're married. It's only the bachelors he detests. He thinks they're all ravening wolves, who do nothing but go around looking for the next person they can swallow up. – It's made me wonder what he was like himself, before he got married. – No, it's the wives I'm scared of. They could hit on ... Oh, yes they could, you know. I hear what they say about other people, so I know what to expect for myself. When a young wife can't display wild affection for her husband, her friends are always waiting to see who she'll fall in love with. Because they consider it inevitable that it must happen to everyone once.'

'So do I.'

'What nonsense!'

'But it's only natural,' he said, throwing himself down onto a chair by the table. 'Either you have been in love, or you are now, or if that's not the case ... well, then you will be. There is nobody who isn't at some point.'

'Oh that's simply nauseating,' she burst out, pulling a face.

He laughed, a touch cynically but not unpleasantly. That laugh revealed the broadness of his mouth, as well as thin, red lips and healthy teeth. Richard Berg looked his best when he smiled, although he seldom did so.

'Are you always that careful?' he asked, regarding her with curiosity. These two reserved individuals had grown accustomed to talking freely to each other about anything. An overt question would always receive an honest answer.

'Equally careful about everything, all the time.'

'But doesn't that impose terrible constraints?'

'Of course it does. But I'm determined not to give them the slightest excuse. You need only look at my groom, I've even thought of him. Have you noticed him?'

An almost imperceptible smile played on her lips.

'Oh yes. Eyes like a cow, nose like a clenched fist, and a mouth that stretches from ear to ear, and pulls lopsidedly up one cheek. An undeniably handsome fellow.'

She laughed at his description, finding it apt.

'I wouldn't find another like him for fifty miles around,' she said with satisfaction, 'And I broke in both him and Prince myself. Prince is doubtless the more intelligent of the two, but I'm proud of Jöns all the same.'

'That shows good taste.'

'I positively revel in his ugliness every time I meet someone when I'm out riding. It lends me such respectability, at least in my own eyes. And he's *married* too.'

Her smile was so much the epitome of spiteful cunning that she felt ashamed of it herself, and dared not look up.

'Well, you can be quite confident where he's concerned. But you know, I think living this sort of life must be very dreary for you out here.'

'Have you found it so?'

'I – oh!' He said no more, but there was no doubt about what he meant. It gave her a feeling of exultant joy.

There was a short pause.

'Do you know, I like Elvira enormously,' she said suddenly and for no apparent reason, 'If I'd been a man, I could have fallen in love with her.'

'Yes, she's charming, but a trifle, um, how shall I put it? ... a trifle naive, which is captivating beyond words in adolescence, but later ... well ... There was something rather like that about you as an adolescent, though in quite a different way. I can see you now, your face when you thought you knew it all, your gangliness. It was the most comical combination you could wish to see ... and you could be so irritating! ... so totally unreasonable. You would never contemplate giving in, however much in the wrong you were.'

'Why should I have given in to *you*?' There was a hint of the old mockery.

'Because I was right.' He looked at her with satisfaction. 'But when all's said and done, perhaps that was precisely what appealed to me. Mama's indulgence of her boy had turned me into a sort of domestic tyrant behind Papa's back; it was so novel to come up against some opposition.'

He fell silent. Selma absent-mindedly let the toe of her shoe play along the hem of her dress, and the doctor had allowed his head to sink onto his chest, a deep furrow forming between his eyebrows.

'Papa didn't realize what a disservice he was doing his son, when he brought you and Kristerson together,' he said abruptly.

'You mean that you and I ...?' Selma turned to the window as if to look out over the park. 'It would never have done, you know.'

'Why not?' came the sharp retort.

Selma stood gazing out with an expression of indifference.

'Because the very fact that it would have given you rights over me would have ruined everything,' she said calmly. 'You're a despot, but what you've always liked about me is that I've dared to stand up to you. If I'd been in your hands and been forced to give in, that would have been the end of that.'

'So, you only believe in free marriage?' he said slowly, and chewed his nails.

'No,' she said quickly, 'Not in the usual sense of the word. I can't see marriage as anything other than basically indissoluble. It should be a union of free, independent individuals and its aim should be their mutual cooperation and growth, not just for a time, but for their whole lives. Not everyone has such high expectations, and most people have to make do with infinitely less; the woman is just a superfluous appendage of the man, and an appendage that is generally nothing in its own right, come to that. As individuals, they have no need of each other; they go their own way, each active in their own sphere, without a care for each other's efforts, except for the results. Children and finances, those are the only things that truly bind them; the wedding and all the rest are purely superficial, a public acknowledgment of what ought to be, but is usually absent ... Yes, you're laughing at me of course, but it doesn't matter! It's such fun to have someone to talk to.'

She turned round and looked at him. He was sitting bent forward, elbows on knees, his gaze fixed on the carpet.

'Go on,' he said. 'It's interesting hearing a woman give her unbiased opinion on this for once. They're generally as petrified of mentioning such matters as they would be of touching a red-hot iron. What more did you have to say?'

She went over and sat down on a chair a little way from him.

'Well, this: there happen to be a few female individuals whose characters are far too strong to allow them to be that kind of appendage to *just any man*, unlike the majority who can manage it. In fact, it's considered in some quarters quite *proper* that way. Oh yes, people talk about liking each other, and so on ... but what sort of basis is that to build on? A liking can come and go, often it's just ... well, it's not worth speaking of. So, those independent women should never marry, or at least not the way things are now. I happen to be one of them, and if Uncle had had a better knowledge of human nature, he would have said: don't ever marry. I might have obeyed him.'

'You would not.'

She cast him a quick sideways look, but made no response to his comment.

'Even if one of those individuals is brought together with a character of the kind that would complement her own,' she went on earnestly in a restrained, matter-of-fact tone, as if trying to remain at a distance from something, 'even then it might not be what a marriage ought to be. Too many conventional attitudes would still be ingrained in him. He'd never forget that legally he was the one with the power. And I mean the sort of power that isn't based on persuasion and a voluntary recognition of his superiority. If she gave herself blindly, he'd soon tire, and if she opposed him, he'd insist on his rights. So it would be a choice between secret loathing and open hostility.'

He looked at her.

'Selma, are you *really* as cold as you act? Don't you ever feel that thirst for happiness, which ... '

She rose suddenly and went over to the window again.

'It makes me sick listening to newly-weds sometimes!' she burst out crossly, 'They imagine that no-one else in the whole world has ever been as happy as them, and yet ...'

'What?'

There was no reply.

He got up and went over to her.

'And yet?' he said gently. 'I'd rather like to ask you a question.'

'No; one should never ask questions,' she answered in a half-whisper, without looking up.

They stood in silence.

'Our Lord was in an unusually good mood one day,' she began with an enigmatic little smile, 'And he wanted to give mankind a gift to enjoy. He scattered a few seeds and let the wind blow them down to earth. And wherever one of the seeds came to rest, a beautiful flower grew. People wanted to give it a name, so they called it happiness. The wise ones amongst them took pleasure in the gift and didn't venture to so much as touch the pink petals, for fear of harming them. But there were also stupid people, and they chopped up the flower along with their cabbage and consumed it, to get the full benefit of it. And what's more, they complained to Our Lord because the cabbage didn't taste nice. There, that's my concept of happiness.'

'Aha, a Platonist!'

He turned on his heel with a scornful laugh.

She pressed her forehead to the window frame with a dejected look, but did not reply.

'But what if you're up to your neck in an immoral liaison, of the kind that enjoys the special protection of the church?'

He threw her a long look over his shoulder, but she was facing away from him, so all he could see was part of one cheek; it turned as red as blood, and he at once regretted his words.

'Then you grit your teeth and look the world brazenly in the face,' she said firmly, 'But if you have any trace of honour left, you don't forget for a moment that you've forfeited all right to – to the very idea of a real marriage.'

It was a wounding reply, and he could have kicked himself in annoyance at having provoked it.

'Have you read the draft of my new book?' he said, hastily casting about for a new topic of conversation.

'Yes. I've even been so bold as to make a few comments.' She turned to face him, and her face had reverted to its usual expression. 'To me, it seems a little too scientific to be truly popular; you assume too much of your readers.'

'Do you think so? Where's the manuscript at the moment?'

'Down in my room; I'll go and fetch it.'

'Can I come with you? I'm rather curious to see your study. Oh, but I forgot ... you wouldn't dare without a chaperone.'

There was something in his tone that offended her.

'As far as I'm concerned, there's absolutely no need for a chaperone; I'm enough of a chaperone for myself,' she answered gloomily. 'But don't you want to have breakfast first?'

'No thank you. I'm like Lord Byron,' he replied with a smile. 'I refuse to be a slave to *any* kind of appetite. Come on.'

Selma lifted her long skirts and preceded him down to the ground floor. At the foot of the stairs she turned to one side, took a key from a little shelf, opened a door and invited him inside.

'Well?' she said triumphantly, once she had closed the door behind them. She felt a real sense of pride. After Black Prince, this was her dearest possession.

He looked around him.

'Imagine, it was just a sort of storeroom or lumber room when I arrived,' she said, with a sort of tenderness, 'and I've gradually made it into this. No-one comes in here except me, and I keep it neat and tidy myself.'

It was a large room, with two sets of windows, only one door, and very thick walls. The furniture was of dark, unpolished oak, upholstered in dark green plush. Everything, from the draped curtains at the windows to the soft carpets, seemed to guarantee silence and tranquillity. It was a room any bookworm would envy.

In the middle of the floor there was a large table, piled with books and portfolios; around it were three or four upright chairs, informally arranged. The walls were lined with bookcases and shelves, and the only ornaments were a pair of bronze statuettes and a few quick sketches, all of heads of horses or dogs. A heavy bronze lamp hung from the ceiling, and was often needed, for even now in the brightest morning light the room appeared dark and gloomy.

'Well?' repeated Selma, when her cousin did not say anything.

'Imagine your never showing me this before!'

'I haven't been using it during your stay, and besides ... I seldom come here except when I want to be alone. I'm afraid of other people getting too used to coming in here; it's so pleasant, that once they got the taste for it, I'm afraid they might never want to be anywhere else.' She gave him a mischievous look.

'Doesn't your husband come in here?'

'Never. He finds it too quiet and dismal.'

The doctor went over to the table and leafed through various things.

'You seem to take your studies very seriously,' he said, looking in one of the books.

She laughed.

'Yes. There's no better use, you know, for the time I have left over from keeping the household machine running. I've no children to educate; I have to make do with educating myself.'

'I wish that people with children would think that way, too.'

'Yes – and incidentally – you ought to give Elvira more of your time; stimulate her interest a little more, so you could feel you had more in common. If not for your own sake or for hers, then you should do it for your little boy.' At these last words, a softness came into her voice, a sort of caress, like stroking one's hand over a silky little head. 'You must remember, his mother will always be the one who gives him his initial guidance, and if she knows no better than to babble nonsense at him, it may affect him all his life. You mustn't overlook the importance of her influence, because you'll never devote as much of your time to him as she will. A man is taken up with his own endeavours and can't immerse himself in anyone else's. But we should all remember that we create the foundations on which coming generations have to build – that our children are the immediate future of mankind. If we lived only for the present moment, we would be no better than animals.'

He gave her a long look.

'Moralizer,' he said softly, with a hint of mischief and derision in his eye.

She flushed a little, as one does when one has been found out.

Then he came across his manuscript on the table, opened it and began to read the comments she had pencilled in the margin. She stood close beside him, her hands resting on the table, following attentively as he read.

'Upon my word – this is very well done indeed!' he exclaimed all at once, 'If I could fathom how ...'

He stopped as a thought struck him. What had driven her to all this? What was it that explained how she always understood him? ... that her attitude of mind ... He looked around the room, which seemed to epitomize her whole evolution, and then at her again. She was aware of it all, felt it in the very way he looked at her, and therefore kept her eyes obstinately fixed on the table.

At that moment, he felt that no beauty in the world could compete with that distinctive, youthful face – that thick, yellow-brown fringe, carelessly pushed to one side, that complexion, which ranged from the sharply defined patch of red to coldest white, with an almost imperceptible hint of creamy yellow, like frosted ivory.

Would he never see that assumed coldness thaw? He *must* see another expression in those grey eyes, knowing now that it was possible.

'Selma,' he said, slowly, huskily, as the warm current invading his senses surged higher and higher and lent his eyes a deeper brilliance.

And then he put his hand on hers, softly and with an almost imperceptible pressure. She did not move, did not lift her eyes from the table, but it was as if the thrilling warmth from that hand flooded her whole being. Her colour deepened still further, and her bosom swelled as she breathed more heavily.

At twenty-three, our blood does not flow very serenely through our veins, and there it was – that temptation to lift her eyes to his, to let all consideration drown in his gaze, and to throw herself to his breast just once and confess that she was not so cold, that she too felt the power of this illicit, exultant passion!

But suddenly she pulled away her hand and took a step back, the folds of her long dress swinging from her slender hips in a single swirl.

Everything inside her was in turmoil at the idea that he could sink to something which, in her eyes, would put him on a par with the man whose tokens of endearment had made his very touch hateful. Everything was profaned, she could not accept even that pressure of a hand without it becoming impure. It was no longer the individual she saw, but what is common to all, which had only ever shown itself to her coarse and naked. She felt disgust.

'Oh – I know you all!' she cried with ruthless brutality, '*couche là*, dog! – that's the only thing that works.' She beat at the empty air with her clenched fist, as if with that single gesture she could have knocked him to the ground.

There was such untrammelled hatred in her cry that he stood there astounded. What had he done?

'*You're* the ones who want to be called strong,' she went on, panting in her haste, 'and you don't possess the slightest power over yourselves! When was it shameful for you to give in to temptation, and when didn't the insult fall on us? Go! I don't want to set eyes on you.'

She threw herself onto a chair and buried her face in her hands.

Making no reply, he took a few paces about the room – that dark room, where the Brussels carpets absorbed every sound of his steps.

He understood her. Perhaps she was right.

He stopped in front of her. The colour had drained from his face.

'Selma,' he said, and she looked up, coldly and sharply.

'Don't you dare, even now?' He held out his big, thin hand, but did not look at her. He did not want to influence her will even by his look. If she could believe him, she ought to do it without the need for words or explanation.

She stood up, and their eyes met, calm and interrogative.

'Oh yes, I dare,' she replied in a voice that did not quaver, and she put her hand in his. He pressed it so hard that it hurt, but without warmth – with only the force of firm resolve.

'Selma,' he said gravely. 'Now I know what you're worth, and I'm almost glad you didn't become my wife: this is infinitely more. I honour you.'

He let go of her hand, turned and left the room.

But she remained, watching the door even after he had closed it.

'Egoism, egoism,' came the mocking echo inside her. 'You knew that *that* would mean losing him.'

Chapter 9

Richard was to set off on his foreign tour directly after leaving Squire Kristerson's. Elvira would accompany him as far as Copenhagen and then return from there to join her mother and young son.

It was the day after the scene in the study, and Selma was up early to supervise the farewell breakfast. She was in a state of painful anxiety and had barely slept all night.

She stood quite alone in the long, gallery-like dining room, with its four windows. The table was set. It glistened with silver and shining glass, and she arranged the last asters of the season in the vase in the table centrepiece.

Her anxiety drove her to feverish activity. She wanted to chase away her thoughts. But everything was ready now, which was why she was busying herself with the flowers.

> 'Asters proudly hold your heads
> where once my roses stood'

ran through her head like a distant, inarticulate melody. She shook her head to get rid of it. Good God, was she going to get sentimental now, as well? And she hated poetry!

But the asters certainly were lovely. She arranged them so the colours went with each other, and they made a magnificent bouquet.

> 'The last lark sings farewell....'

Oh, for goodness sake. What was all that old sentimentality to her? She lashed out with her hand as if at a swarm of whining mosquitoes. Then she took a few steps back to see how the table looked. The colourful flowers lent it the air of a party – a farewell party! She put her hands over her ears to block the sound of the unthinking, monotonous rhythm:

> 'My cold and lovely memories,
> mimic the roses once more!'

What banality! No, she *must* put a stop to this! She flushed as if at an insult, and recklessly reached forward and gathered up the flower heads in her hand, crushing them together in blind rage. It was as if she needed to take her revenge on something, and she took pleasure in feeling the dewy petals crumple in her clenched hand.

She pulled the bouquet from the vase as if seizing the severed head of an enemy, and with clenched teeth she opened the window and threw it, crushed and spoilt, to the winds.

Flowers ... affectation ... hollow phrases! Away with it all! – Why was it so difficult to stay sober?

She shut the window and felt calmer. But there was a weight on her mind. She could not keep still, and yet could not leave the room. Some presentiment told her that Richard would seek her out there. It would never have entered her head to try to avoid him. Why should she? Now they both knew ... What? A thought for which there was no word fine and pure enough ... something silent and secret, something huge and rich ...

She ran her hands over her cheeks, which felt cold, then went over to the sideboard and looked at herself in the mirror. How pale she was! She rubbed her face until it was flaming, but the blood sank back at once, like the mercury in a thermometer; and even her hands seemed whiter than usual. She began walking up and down the long, narrow floorboards. She thought that might give her some colour. What would Richard think? Consider her weak and foolish ... oh!

Just then she heard his steps outside; he entered briskly, taking out his watch as he shut the door. Selma looked over to the ornamental clock – three quarters of an hour left. Her heart was suddenly in her mouth, and she felt her face grow cold. Now they were to part – to part!

'Elvira's still packing,' he said, coming up to her and giving her his hand. 'I wanted to say goodbye to you first.'

It sounded as though he intended to add something, but he stopped, released her hand and went over to the window.

She felt robbed of all breath.

'I thought we might have something to say to each other,' he went on in a strange monotone, without turning round. One hand drummed nervously on a little table that stood by the window.

Selma went up to him.

'Richard,' she said lightly. She felt such a need to say something, but did not know what. She could see how upset he was.

Then he turned to face her and they looked at each other – two pale faces without a trace of weakness, but with the same expression in their features of bitter struggle against emotion, of violently suppressed suffering. They were so dissimilar in looks, he so dark and she so fair, but just for a moment there was a striking resemblance between them. It vanished almost at once, as Selma regained her composure.

It pained her to see him suffering too. She had no time to think of her own grief, for now she could feel only his.

'Richard, it will pass,' she said, putting her hand on his as it rested on the table. 'It's only now it feels like this; when you get out into the world and form new relationships, you'll forget it in no time.'

He looked at her, mortified. To think how *she* must be feeling, yet here she was comforting him! What a wretch he was!

It was as if she could tell what he was thinking.

'And I want to thank you for all that you've taught me over the years, for every letter you've written and for every kind word,' she said, applying pressure with her cold fingers to his big hand, which felt burning hot and lay so passively under hers.

'Have you no regrets? Wouldn't you like it all undone – like to have that time back, but with me rubbed out?' he said, equally flatly and with the same tormented expression on his face.

She considered for a moment, in order to give an honest answer. Should she wish that she could give back those years of happiness and growth, because she now had to pay for them so dearly?

'No, never,' she said, with a smile so wan and frank that it cut him to the quick. Her attempt to look glad merely tortured him further. He could not look at her.

'This is revenge on me for having always denied it,' he broke out. 'I tried to claim it was over – even to myself. But it wasn't. It was pure conceit to imagine any such thing. Why ... *why* didn't I take you from him!'

It was a frenzied, violent outburst, and he squeezed her hand as hard as if he had been a patient under the surgeon's knife.

'Go out onto the veranda – or have a drink of water – or anything, but calm yourself,' she said. 'Or what about some brandy?" She was about to fetch it.

'No,' he said, 'just give me time.'

Softly and tenderly, she stroked his hand, which had now relinquished its tight grip; and it was as if he were swallowing his emotion in great draughts.

'I never thought it could have such power over me,' he said, taking a deep breath as if he were exhausted. 'But of course, time's a great healer.'

He took out his handkerchief and mopped his brow several times.

'Musset knew it: *On ne badine pas avec l'amour*,' he said, with an autumnal smile.

They stood for a moment without speaking.

'Shall we write to one another?' he said suddenly, with one of his abrupt changes of mood. His tone was almost businesslike.

'No. You shall hear from me through Elvira; she and I plan to be frequent correspondents.'

He made no reply. The decision was hers.

'Go out into the garden now, and take a brisk walk,' she said. 'You don't want people to see this in our faces, do you?'

'All right, I will,' he said in a more natural voice, and pressed her hands. 'Goodbye then, Selma. And thanks for everything, you honourable soul. We're still fumbling and searching, but what binds the two of us is that we both have an unshakeable conviction that there's something worth searching *for*.'

His sharp features seemed to brighten, and he made no attempt to hide the moisture that was glistening in his eyes.

He went out.

By the time Elvira came in, Selma was standing uncorking the bottles of wine, as composed and efficient as usual – with something of the frosty morning about her.

Elvira's hair was crimped and powdered. She was looking exceptionally nice today.

'How grand, like a real special occasion!' she cried, looking at the table. There was something young and soft and warm about her, and as she went up to Selma and kissed her, the latter could not help tenderly stroking her hair, as one might a pretty child's. Elvira's answer was to look up into her face with such devoted admiration that Selma's habitual reserve melted away; she hugged the young woman to her.

'You're a dear little girl,' she said gaily.

Her laugh sounded a little like a sob, but Elvira could not see it, for her face was buried against Selma's shoulder.

'Now go and fetch your husband; he's out in the garden. It's high time we were having breakfast, and I shall call Paul,' said Selma, releasing her.

'Yes, but don't you think he could well have taken me on his trip abroad?' whispered Elvira, but without looking up, because her eyes were filling with tears. 'If you were to ask him, he'd agree.'

'No, he can't afford it. And in any case, it's best this way.'

An element of coolness came into Selma's voice, and Elvira looked sulky at not finding support. She patted her fringe into place, and went out to find Richard.

Half an hour later, the Squire and Selma stood on the steps waving, as the carriage pulled away.

'It will feel empty to you, my little wife,' said the Squire kindly, as they went back into the house.

'It certainly will, at first,' replied Selma impassively; then she took the key from the shelf and went into her own room, while the Squire went on up the stairs.

She had not been in this room since the previous day, when she had showed it to Richard, and recently she had not often bothered to come here, because she had put her studies aside. This whole summer had been one long sunny day. And now the sky had suddenly darkened.

She crossed the soft carpet to the table. She wanted to arrange it for some kind of work, but could not touch those papers and books. She felt a suffocating pressure on her chest and tore at the buttons of her bodice to undo a few and try to get some air. It was no use.

Tears? No, there were no tears. They had stood there on the steps and exchanged platitudes. Is that how they would remember each other? That trite 'Thank you for having us' and 'Have a good journey.' Oh – anything but that! Would he remember her as one among a dozen others?

She went down to the stables, where Jöns was polishing tack.

'My horse – this instant! And you will stay at home,' she said brusquely.

She made her way back, calmly, with measured steps, although every nerve in her body was quivering with impatience and her heart was pounding as if it might burst. Would she get there in time, would she get there in time?

Jöns watched her go in astonishment. He had never known anything like it: 'My horse – and *you* will stay at home!' And her tone – as if she were talking to a dog!

But Jöns was a dutiful soul, and within five minutes he had led Prince to the steps. Selma was just coming out with her crop in her hand and her riding cap on her head. She did not normally wear it except in the paddock, but today she was heading for the road.

Jöns stood open-mouthed for a moment before he could pull himself together enough to return to the stables where his horse was whinnying for its companion.

Selma did not follow the road for more than a short distance before she let Prince jump a hollow and set off over stubble and newly ploughed fields at a speed perilous to both herself and her horse. She was heading for a wooded slope visible in the distance, and she shunned neither ditches nor fences; that was where the road ran, after sweeping round in a wide loop.

Prince grew more eager with every step; she could feel his muscles tauten, the dirt splashed high up her dress as they crossed some boggy ground, but it did not worry her; only onward, onward! She could hear nothing but hoof beats and her own panting breath. Now and then a horseshoe rang against a stone or the leather of the saddle creaked with the tension of the girth.

The energetic motion set her blood coursing, and her cheeks were burning. No more whingeing! How glorious to be alive!

At a gallop they went up the slope between the great oaks, but then they met hazel bushes growing more densely, and were forced to slow to a walk. She would get there in time, even so. Every so often she had to bend down and free her dress, which had caught on some thorny branch.

There, she was at the top, and could see the road.

She paused and listened. The sound of a carriage could be heard below. They would not be able to see her until they reached the crown of the hill, as she had stationed herself just where the road began to descend again. The sand crunched beneath the wheels. The coach came slowly up the hill. She urged the horse round in a circle and then brought him to a halt in a small clearing among the bushes.

The animal's flanks moved beneath her as he panted, and she felt her blood surging with the beat of her pulse. She pushed back her cap to cool her brow; her hair felt damp when she pushed it off her face. What a ride! She patted her horse on its lathered neck, and the sound echoed down the hill.

With one firm movement she pulled her jacket down taut at the waist, supported the hand holding the riding crop against her right knee and then sat motionless in the saddle. She felt so free and happy, so young and vital.

Black Prince raised his intelligent head, twitched his ears and looked towards the road.

The carriage was approaching.

Richard, who had been sitting slumped in one corner of the carriage, suddenly sat bolt upright and the coachman reined in the horses.

'No, drive on!' called Selma. She smiled at Elvira, waved her riding crop in greeting, and as the carriage drove away she backed the horse, took a flying leap over the ditch, and joined the road.

'Goodbye!' they shouted after each other, and she set off for home at a brisk trot, while the carriage slowly continued down the hill and disappeared from view.

They had exchanged only a single glance – a mutual, inaudible cry of encouragement, but because it was so unexpected, the vibrant tableau had been all the more striking, and somehow etched itself in the memory. Richard would always remember her thus.

Her bosom looked higher and her waist smaller, because she was always tight-laced under her riding habit. The black cloth was moulded around her strong arms and the attractive curve of her shoulders. Her cheeks were patches of vivid red, making her brow and chin seem paler than ever; her nostrils flared with her heavy breathing, and beneath the thin lines of her eyebrows, her light eyes were full of spirit and zest for life. She was hot and sweating, her horse matted and wet, and her skirt spattered with yellow clay. There was no sensibility here to the need to stay neat, no soft charm, only the robust beauty of health, which can only be perceived by an eye open to nature.

What a splendidly theatrical effect! thought Selma with scorn as she trotted along the road, don't I just know how well I look on horseback. It's a wonder I didn't arrange for some Bengal lights too!

In her annoyance with herself, she gave Prince a lash. Nor did he get his bread that day, although he stood watching her with great, reproachful eyes, until Jöns lost patience and led him away.

When Selma had changed her dress, she did not go down to

her study. She found it impossible. She felt homeless, alien, lost. Everything seemed suddenly so aimless and empty. How would she endure it? How, how?

The moment she stepped inside the house, all her earlier desolation returned, but heavier, more hopeless and resigned than before.

She went into the drawing room. The whole suite of rooms lay deserted. Loneliness was tangibly settling over those rich apartments, as the dust settles in an empty house – from out of nowhere, it seems, but incessantly, inexhaustibly, in forlorn silence.

Ah, life would never, ever subside into its old rut again!

She sank down onto a sofa and pressed her forehead against her clasped hands on the cushions.

All her thoughts had, to a greater or lesser extent, revolved around him. There had been no time for brooding or doubt. Getting close to him had been the aim, winning his approval had been the reward. She had been walking blindfold, believing that it was the desire for knowledge leading her on, and life had seemed so rich.

But now it was over. She was to take her poor rags and go. She had been living on stolen property, on a lie, she – who had wanted to be so honest! It had been sheer delusion! Aah!

She gave a long, moaning sigh.

Then resentment began to assert itself – vexation at being so cowardly, at allowing herself to be crushed by the slightest thing, she who owned everything for which other people strive: money, freedom, power. Was that not cowardly?

She sat up violently and threw her head back against the arm of the sofa.

Away with all these mawkish feelings, go, go! It was only a matter of shaking them off.

But then the dissent flared up, for something inside her was stronger than she. It frightened and pursued, lured and caressed, it left no room for a single thought, it was all-encompassing. She covered her ears, but it grew in defiance; it shrieked, exulted, lamented, implored; it knew every succession of notes, it mastered every variation, and it was all-encompassing: the very thing from which she wanted to free herself. She fought it and threw it forcibly aside; it was there again, many times stronger.

Was she then so weak, so pathetically weak, that she could not wrench it from her heart?

The sense of powerlessness brought with it anguish, gripping her in its teeth and claws. Her self-confidence was shaken, she was worn down by the inner battle, and felt herself go hot and cold with almost superstitious anxiety.

But she *could* not give in! If the act of will was not enough in itself, then there must be other ways: new relationships, new surroundings, travel and distractions.

She got quickly to her feet and went into her husband's room. He was lying on the sofa reading the newspapers, that is to say, asleep. Awoken by the noise Selma made with the door, he hurriedly took up his paper, which had slipped to the floor with the hand that held it.

'Paul, I have a favour to ask you,' she began directly, seating herself on a chair beside the sofa.

The Squire looked up with a mixture of delight and alarm. What favour could *she* have to ask?

A momentary, guarded look came into her eyes, but was immediately gone. Did he suspect? Yes, something – anything but the truth. Just a woman's whim.

'It's something I want so terribly,' she said in a low voice, bending forward to rest her elbows on her knees and absentmindedly clasping and unclasping her hands.

She fell silent, as if she dared not continue.

The Squire's imagination ran away with him into the wildest speculations, but he too remained silent. Although he was afraid of what she might suggest, he longed for her to speak again, for there was something in her tone of voice which ...

'Yes, you'll no doubt think it very childish, but I've got it into my head now.' It seemed to be the voice of someone different, not Selma, so soft did it sound. The Squire would have liked to pull her to him, caressing, murmuring, but he felt a vague sense of apprehension. After all, it must be something completely out of the question, as *she* was asking! The uncertainty burnt and goaded him. He was quite convinced that it was something to which he would have to say no, but what would he not have given to be able to say yes and see her face light up with devoted gratitude. What *could* it be?

There was a sense of something held in check when he spoke; his eyes were buried in his newspaper, and Selma was on the verge of finding him attractive in earnest.

'What is it you want so badly?' he said.

'Well, you see, it really has felt dreadfully empty since Elvira and Richard went ... '

She fell silent.

'And so?'

'I've never been to Stockholm.'

'Is *that* what you want?'

'Yes.'

'Is that all?' He laughed with a profound sense of relief. 'I expect that can be arranged.'

'Yes, but I want it to be now.'

'When?'

Now came the hardest part. She smiled, but her lips trembled nervously as she leant forward and put her arm round his neck.

'Tomorrow,' she whispered.

He gave a start, and let his paper fall to the floor.

'But my dear child, just think ...'

'Oh, Paul, it's easily done. I shall arrange everything, but I can't wait, I'm longing for it so terribly. You *must* do it.'

She laughed even more nervously, trying to look carefree, and shook him by the shoulders.

'Yes, but ...'

'No, not *but*, just *yes*!' she cried.

'But you must see ...'

'That you can't possibly say anything but yes!' She gave a loud laugh, and put both arms around his neck for a moment. He could not recall ever having seen her so happy and excited, he thought.

'Yes,' he said, and looked up into her face with the eyes of a man in love.

The next day, they caught the express train.

It was with a certain reverence that Selma ascended the wide steps of the National Gallery for the first time. She worshipped art with a kind of uncritical admiration, and this seemed to her like a temple.

Living in Skåne, she was naturally very familiar with all the art galleries of Copenhagen, but here it was all new to her.

It amazed her that the Squire could remain so unmoved as he entered, tramping along in his usual placid way on his big, broad, country squire's feet, always putting the heel down first and letting the toes follow along with a rolling motion. Not a sign of elasticity, just the weight of a mammoth.

'Oh, look, Loki and Sigyn!' she cried, pulling him by the arm, and she felt so utterly disappointed when he stared at the picture with such a dull and quizzical look; she was familiar with most of the pictures here from photographs, it was like renewing old acquaintances and she scarcely needed the catalogue. She pulled her hand away, for it seemed that he had no idea what this was all about, and so they moved on to the next room.

'Oh, look Paul, a Wickenberg!' she cried. 'Just think, this is the first time I've actually seen one!'

She suddenly fell silent and let her arms fall. Then she took a few steps to the side and stopped. Her eyes were fixed on a picture hanging high up near the ceiling.

A man in black velvet, lying dead on the floor, the face seen from behind the top of the head, foreshortened.

Richard! She felt a stab of recognition. It was his crooked nose, his shaggy black hair, it was more than that: his mercurial nature, captured in those ghastly, greenish-white features.

This picture was a sphinx, binding her with its secret power.

She looked it up in her catalogue to find some explanation. 'Epilogue,' it said. The picture was to speak for itself.

Yes, every detail had something to tell. The tablecloth, which the dead man had almost pulled off as he fell; the medallion there with its chain; roses which had dropped and scattered their petals – and his broken blade: the last thing to betray his faith.

In Selma's imagination it became a whole story, and the picture was merely the epilogue. She dreamt her way through scene after scene, seeing everything as if it had really come to life. It was sunny and warm, and the grass was as smooth as velvet. The water came cascading down from a height, arching out on every side, glittering in the sun, and falling with a splash into its peaceful pool. Silk rustled between the trees and from an arbour came the sound of laughter ...

She gave a start.

'Do you think it beautiful?' said the Squire.

'No.'

As she said no more, he went over to the hunting nymph, where he in turn became captivated.

In her mind's eye, Selma went back to the story the picture had to tell. Now the scene was the hall – dark-polished panelling and tables with silver and crystal; wine, to add sparkle to the senses, and the most exquisite roses, fresh with morning dew. Then came the quarrel ... the quarrel over a woman. He was the rejected one. That was why he was lying there stiff and cold. And they had all gone, cowardly or crowing ... left him ... fled ...

Should the woman not have loved all that is unlovely and dismal, looking in death more dismal still? Was it not precisely that which demanded love and sunshine? That bitter resentment, frozen in those desolate features, how easily it could have turned into pliancy and warmth! And this cold woman had not understood that all the happiness in the world was as nothing compared to *that* ...

By the end she felt as though she were standing in the picture herself – not grieving and crying but dumb, in hopeless despair that happiness had not come, and that now it was too late. And she could throw herself down on the carpet among the flower-petals, wringing her hands until the joints cracked and stare ... just stare dry-eyed at that face.

'Well *I* think it's ugly,' said the Squire, who had come back over.

'Lord, yes – it is ugly,' she said, waking up with a shiver and turning round. She was deathly pale, and mopped her brow with her handkerchief.

'What would make anyone want to paint something like that?' observed the Squire.

'Yes, it is peculiar,' she answered dully, and moved away. But that face haunted her – insistent, like her rebellious senses, accusing her as they did – even now it was all over.

She wandered around aimlessly; nothing interested her now. At the entrance to one of the side galleries she stopped nonetheless, but this time it was not a work of art which caught her attention; it was a bit of real life.

Two artists had taken sole possession of the room; there were few visitors in the National Gallery that day. There was a young man and a young girl. Neither of them noticed Selma, so engrossed were they in a lively discussion.

He was busy copying a picture. Her easel stood further off, but she had left her work and come up to his. The latter was clearly the subject of their dispute.

He had a stained old coat, a downy, newly-grown beard and a carefree young face.

She was not much to look at, but had a nice figure. Her dress was made of a cheap material, but the outfit had style, and it suited her. She spoke quickly and quietly with a sing-song intonation, holding her palette in one hand and a paintbrush in the other. He sat listening to her with a smile; it was clear that he was making fun of her comments. But she was too spirited to let that stop her. She laughed, too, but kept on talking, gesticulating eagerly with the handle of her brush; when she had reached her final point, she drew a rapid stroke in the air as though it were a conductor's baton, cast him an exhilarated look of appeal, and returned to her work. He sat watching her as she crossed the floor with a rather wilful air and a slight swing of her hips. Then he took a rag from his paintbox and firmly wiped something out of his picture.

Selma could have laughed out loud at this little scene which she had covertly observed, and the fresh air from this fragment of real life dispelled for a moment the suffocating weight which had descended on her senses. But when she saw the two of them immersing themselves in their work as earnestly as if their lives or their daily bread depended on it, she felt a gnawing envy and could not bear it. Dreams for her future, buried long ago, rose up and came back to haunt her.

'Let's go this way instead,' she said to the Squire, who was standing dutifully in front of a picture and finding it all most tedious.

They turned and wandered round again from room to room. But Selma took no interest in the pictures; she was busy thinking of all those people who had lived and died, leaving behind them a thought, an achievement, their mark. Even the workmen who had laid the tiles on the floor ... But she? To vegetate and die – that was to be her life. Nothing to show for it, be it long or short. To vegetate and die – calmly and acquiescently.

She thought of the girl in there: poor, but free to strive. And she herself – did she not own precisely what others strive for by working? – money ... Money? – what a poor word! Money, but nothing to strive for. No, to do battle with life, to fight for your bread, that's living.

She passed her hand slowly across her brow.

To vegetate and die, that was a duty of course – for her.

She gave a start as, happening to look to one side, she caught sight of a picture of medium size, hanging in the middle of a wall, excellently lit. It was an old acquaintance. But she had not expected to find it here. She had thought it had been sold abroad.

As it was, it brought a flood of old memories. It was a feeling that fused together the past and the present, she lost her footing and was swept away.

It was the same picture, and yet so different from the rough, colourless copy she had admired that other time.

Against the background of her memories, the picture now had a double effect; she stopped in surprised silence, looking and looking.

The moon was shining over the water, and far away in the distance the outline of a dark ruin could just be seen. Billowing waves rose slowly, advanced with a caressing breath, sank back with a melancholy sigh, to return again and again with their long, muffled beat. Sea-green shadows slid darkly over the depths, streaks of light stretched away in billowing motion, and beneath their transparent cover of waves, the daughters of the sea lay dreaming, listening to the music of the water-sprite.

One was more beautiful than the rest. With her arm beneath her head, she lay stretched out on her swaying bed. Her gaze was fixed on the sky, where the moon peeped out from behind a thin cloud, casting its light on her soft features. As dreamy as a woman's and as innocent as a child's, that gaze seemed one endless, wondering question.

From Selma's memory came a sound like a forgotten note ... one recognizes it, is touched, is moved ... so distant, yet so pure! Oh God, then she had been a child. And now, now ... !

Not a muscle moved in her face as the tears ran, and every drop released a part of something that had been bound and stunted. Everything that has lain in the earth as if dead, will yet shoot up one day in wind and sun, grow in fair weather and foul; it may be a weed or it may be a crop, but it is healthy and strong – once summer comes.

'Good heavens! Whatever is the matter?' exclaimed the Squire, who had been standing looking at Cain and Abel, and had just returned.

'Nothing,' she replied, wiping her face. 'But come, let's go home.'

'Go? But we haven't seen a quarter of it!'

'I can't take in any more.'

Now her voice failed her.

He made no reply, merely looked surprised, and so they left.

When they reached the entrance of the hotel, Selma stopped.

'I feel so out of sorts,' she said, 'I think I'll go across to Kungsträdgården for a short walk.'

'By all means,' he said kindly, offering her his arm once more.

She had hoped to be able to go alone; it would have felt like taking a good, deep breath. These last few days they had been together constantly – always in each other's company, day and night. She felt it like the effort of carrying a small burden; it is nothing in itself, but with every minute that passes, the longing to set it down for a moment grows, and finally it becomes unendurable.

She leant on his arm more heavily than usual, and he liked that, unaware that she did it because she felt rather weak, as if convalescent after an illness. Nor did she have the normal briskness in her step that usually made it so difficult for her to match her pace to his.

They reached the tree-lined gravel walks without exchanging a word. He had tried to speak, but she had replied only yes and no, so he said no more. He was cast her a long, quizzical look. She was looking straight ahead, and seemed to have forgotten his existence.

'You're always thinking about things,' he said peevishly, 'you'll soon be a mystery no-one can solve.'

'Don't you ever think about things?' she asked, with a smile that rendered the answer all but superfluous.

'No. What would be the point?'

She did not answer, and they sank back into silence again.

'Going to the theatre tonight will cheer you up,' said the Squire after a while, but Selma did not appear to have heard him.

She was brooding on her own state of mind and the discoveries she was making filled her with distaste. Her emotions were intensified to the point of sentimentality, her nerves were on edge, and when she suddenly caught sight of a dark beard on a street corner, she gave a start and her heart began to race.

It had certainly been worth coming all this way to forget!

For a moment, she wished she could have talked to her husband about it. But she realized at once that it was impossible; it would only enrage him, and *that* would be no help to her, merely drive them further apart.

No, she must fight on alone, and she would. There was no other solution: she *had* to conquer it. There was only one way – *work*.

Chapter 10

The Squire opened the door to their room and let Selma enter. He would never have dreamt of preceding his wife. The candles were lit, and over in one corner, supper was laid: a cold collation, grapes and champagne.

Selma gave a start.

'What's this for?' she said with displeasure, indicating the bottles of wine.

'My little wife has been looking so down in the mouth these last few days.'

'What of it?'

'Wine gladdens the human heart.'

She did not reply, but threw her coat and her lace mantilla impatiently onto a chair. So the moment of decision was already here!

'You eat; I can't,' she said in a tired voice, pulling off her long gloves.

She had worn an evening gown of black velvet and brocade to the theatre. Its only adornment was a serpent of dull gold, twining once around the high military collar. The dangling snake's head formed a sort of medallion and its diamond eyes flashed in the candlelight.

'But I ordered it all for you,' said the Squire, looking over at the delicacies.

'Can't help that.'

'But I told the waitress she could leave it all here – it's more pleasant without her running in and out. You may find your appetite.'

'No.'

She shuddered, looking sickened.

'Didn't you enjoy your evening?'

'Oh yes.'

'You look very unhappy about it.'

'It was hot and I got a headache.'

She crossed to one of the windows, lifted the curtain and looked over to the Royal Palace and its waterside terraces. The lamps were reflected in the water, and it felt like a breath of refreshing air to look out on the cold night.

'You eat, Paul, I can't,' she repeated, letting the curtain drop back into place.

The Squire gave a sigh and sat down at the table.

Selma remained standing by the window, playing absent-mindedly with her closed fan. Her complexion was not as clear as usual, and it made her features less attractive. Her sharp chin and thin lips could sometimes give her face a cold, rather repellent look, especially when it was as pale as it was now.

'The caviare's excellent,' said the Squire, 'Won't you try it? It will give you an appetite.'

'No thank you.'

She was seated now, looking idly at one of her hands as it rested on the window-frame – a large, shapely hand, with firm, slender nails. It looked as though it would be able to get properly to grips with what was to come. Then she lifted her eyes and looked at her husband. He appeared engrossed in tackling a lobster.

The Squire was fifty-one now, and he looked his age; a slackness had appeared around the mouth since he had acquired false teeth, and his hair was thinning.

'Why is the law so unjust, that it doesn't let a man marry until he's twenty-one, but lets a woman do it at sixteen?' she said suddenly.

'The law wants to show courtesy to the ladies.'

'Oh no,' she burst out impatiently, gently tapping her fan against her knee. 'I don't mean that! I mean that we shouldn't be allowed to marry until we've reached our majority, either.'

'A woman matures sooner than a man.'

'I see. So she is capable of taking her own future into her hands earlier? I didn't know that.'

'And there are many who wish to be married before they are twenty-one. Take you, for example.' He smiled good-naturedly and raised his beer glass.

'That's why the law ought to be changed.'

'A woman below the age of majority has the safeguard of requiring the assent of her guardian.'

'But how in the world is a guardian to decide whether she feels any sense of lifelong fellowship with the man who proposes to her, when she doesn't know it yet herself? When she can't even be said to have any true substance to her life.'

'Substance to her life? Nonsense! Many a women lives to reach sixty, without necessarily needing any substance to her life. Idiotic modern ideas! Let her get married first and her life will have substance soon enough: a house and home to run. You saw how it was yourself.'

'Houses and homes would be better run, if women were able to use those four or five years to learn what it entails,' she said, raising her hand and resting her head in it, regarding him with something akin to the dull resignation felt by someone completing a job of work which they have long known to be pointless, but yet feel duty bound to finish. 'What's more, you are forgetting how important those very years between sixteen and twenty usually are for one's inner development.'

It seemed to her that she had had this conversation a hundred times before, although she was raising the topic for the first time. But it must be because she knew his thoughts as well as one knows a book one has learnt by heart: one knows what the answer will be before the question is even posed.

'You're forgetting that in some cases, a speedy marriage is ...' The Squire coughed.

'Laws aren't written for the exceptional cases. And the fact that such things can happen shouldn't cause the law to let two beings who are spiritually mere minors tie themselves to each other for a whole, long life. I still ask the same question.'

'But you don't deny, do you, that a woman generally matures

earlier than a man?'

'In terms of intellect, absolutely not. At least, not with current methods of upbringing. She grows precocious. But that's all. She's always thinking what a grown-up young lady she is. That she could be a married woman any day.' Selma pulled a face.

'I don't see what you have to complain about. You were only sixteen yourself when you married, and it worked out jolly well.'

She flushed a fiery red, and drew herself up in her seat.

'I believe you need only recall what an objectionable creature I was, to realize the absurdity of the situation,' she replied sharply.

'For me, you were the most truly delightful little objectionable creature, and looking at you now, it's hard to believe that early marriage does any harm. You really have grown into a fine woman.' He looked at her with something akin to the delight a sportsman might feel on contemplating an elegant thoroughbred.

'You should never have said that!' She stood up and threw her fan onto the console table, where it landed with a clatter onto the mirrored top. This was a new conversation, and the time for composure was past. 'Does no harm – oh! – does no harm? What did you think I was, when we married? A poor child, who knew neither herself nor others, who didn't know what was going to happen to her and who was ready to embrace the whole world, because she viewed everything with the same naive ignorance. Tell me, didn't you ever feel sorry for me? Unlike the others, I had no mother to tell me ...'

'Do you think mothers talk about those things?'

The Squire picked his teeth idly.

'Surely it ought to be their duty?' She looked at him in surprise.

'If that is how you intended to bring up your children, then the Lord did well not to let you have any,' said the Squire, abruptly tossing down his crumpled napkin. 'The duty of mothers is normally to see that their daughters grow up as pure and ...'

She gave a strangled cry, 'Aargh, I can't stand hearing any more of this. Don't you see that my profound loathing of anything dirty comes *precisely from* knowing how dirty it is!

And of course I didn't know it before. Oh, it's wretched! We go about conjuring up such a beautiful picture for ourselves – all flowers and sunshine – and thinking that everything's as it is in our own minds! Oh God! ... we're like mankind before the Fall – so blissful and ignorant. We can't see the difference between good and evil.'

'Oh yes, and I suppose the lot of you ought to know all about it, just like ...' He spoke crossly and with growing irritation.

'Just like you men,' she supplied. 'Yes, exactly.'

It sounded so conclusive, and was said in something approaching her old tone.

'Oh no, there must be some morality,' he said loftily, lighting his cigar.

'Yes. The same for us as for you.'

The Squire merely drew on his cigar. She was making one of her absurd demands again, of course, but it seemed rather awkward to point it out to her just now. You never get anywhere with womenfolk; they always have to have the last word. He also knew from experience that once she seized on something, she rarely let go. The discussion was making him feel rather uncomfortable. He would have much preferred to sidestep it.

'When you married me, I was a minor,' she said. Her state of mental stress was making her heart beat fast, but her words were as expressionless as if she had been quoting a section of the lawbook; she had turned them over in her mind so often. 'A promissory note I had written would have been invalid, and no other person had the right to draw one up in my name for the tiniest sum, nor to give away any of what would become mine in the future. My person is more than my money. If I wasn't mature enough to manage my money, then I was certainly less capable still of making decisions about myself. A minor should no more be allowed to pawn her future than her possessions. That's a simple piece of logic.'

'Yes, well, let's not argue. You're in a bad mood. Come and have a glass of champagne, that'll cheer you up.'

'No. I don't want your champagne,' she said in a hard voice. She would have found it repellent at the best of times, but the fact that he could make such a suggestion just now, when she was finally speaking of what had been fermenting inside her all these years, merely increased her bitterness.

But he felt warm and amply fed, and as he had only vaguely followed what she had been saying, he could not know what was about to happen.

'Go on, you're tired,' he persisted, 'Try some, it's refreshing. And grapes! You usually like those.'

'Stop it. I won't touch a thing.'

He did not answer, but worked the cork loose until it flew into the air with a pop. She remained over by the window, motionless, watching him, and two fine lines appeared between her eyebrows, as they always did when she was angry. The Squire filled both glasses, then went over and tried to give one to her, but she pushed away his hand so violently that some of the wine spilt.

'What do you think you're doing!' he said indignantly, setting her glass back on the table, and draining his own. But then he restrained himself, knowing that anger from his side only made her more truculent.

Once he had retrieved the cork and forced it back into the bottle again, he took a seat over on the rocking chair, where he could see her. Emotion had restored to her cheeks those sharply delineated patches of red which made them look faintly rouged. He thought her beautiful. It was that freshness, which ...

She could think only of how there is nothing more repulsive than seeing the passions of youth haunting an old face.

'You're cold, you're frozen, come here and let me warm you up,' he said, spreading his arms, his cigar poised elegantly between two fingers.

'I only wanted to say this: that the vow I made as a child is not binding on me as a woman.'

'What sort of nonsense is that?'

'I can't go on – do you understand – it's over.'

'Are you mad? What silly whim is this?'

He had risen from his chair, but sat down again at once.

'It's not a whim,' she said, leaning against the window frame and shifting her feet a little, as if to avoid the tiring discomfort of standing for so long, 'it's happened slowly, step by step as it were, and it's taken several years to develop. At first it was just an instinctive feeling, and I tried to combat it by lecturing myself on duty and all that. But gradually the distaste was joined by something else – it was shame, in fact.' She spoke calmly and dispassionately, as if the matter concerned someone other than the two of them, for this was all so familiar to her, these were things she must have discussed with herself a hundred times, and she did not hesitate over a single word. 'Every allusion to our marital relations made me wish the ground would swallow me up, and that fact alone proves that there was something unnatural about it all – that things weren't as they should be, because a wife who is fond of her husband doesn't feel ashamed: I expect she feels proud. But by trying to rationalise the shame away, I was forced to think, and then it was all over! What had been a suspicion before awakened into full consciousness. And under the acute stress of it all I couldn't even hint at my emotional state without it provoking you. So I learnt to keep quiet, and we became strangers. Submission was the price of my daily bread, of the luxury, of all the money I had at my disposal, and that "you *must*, because he's paying" made my distaste all the more intense.'

'A fine thing for a wife to be telling her husband!' he exclaimed.

She looked at him, and the shadow of a melancholy smile stole over her face.

'I know I could speak of this for all eternity without your ever understanding me,' she said gravely. 'But I want to say it, even so – not for your sake, but for mine – not because you'll grasp what I'm saying, but because I can't say it to anyone else but you. And just this once, I shall speak my mind. Come what may!'

'You've no right to raise such matters. If everyone thought the way you do, the world would crumble, and no form of society could survive.'

'But I'm not speaking for everyone, only for *myself*,' she said rapidly. 'Because I feel the way I do. I'm fighting for my own cause, because I'm the only one affected by it. But if anyone else feels as I do, if she's selling herself for ready money and doing it day after day, yet without her feminine sensibilities raising any objections, then she has sunk lower than I have now. Then she has fallen like me, but lacks the will to raise herself up. That's all I know.'

'What kind of madhouse talk is that?' The Squire went even redder in the face than before. 'Selling ... What about the marriage ceremony then, if women are going to use that argument whenever they see fit – against their own husbands?'

'The marriage ceremony gives a legal right, but not a moral one. Are you so steeped in prejudice that you can't grasp such a simple thing? If we give ourselves on anything other than equal terms, then we're loose and fallen. It can never be a person's duty to submit to expressions of affection against which their whole being is in revolt. For there *are* no duties contrary to nature.'

'These are remarkable opinions you're expressing all of a sudden,' he said sarcastically, the rage boiling within him.

'All of a sudden?' she echoed, giving a bitter smile and shaking her head with a look of disgust. 'Oh! If there had been any satisfaction to be gained from all this, I might still have felt I had carried out a duty. That would have been some consolation. But there was none to be had. Only shame – bitter, degrading shame, and with it the effrontery of a whispered: Everyone else does it too. The church's blessing gives us the right to sell ourselves. It has the monopoly. Oh, can anything baser be imagined? If you had any conception of how we sink – sink irretrievably! It's utterly appalling. Any respect shown to us seems nothing but a cruel mockery.'

She had let her head sink, and her eyes stared blankly out into space. The timbre had gone from her voice, as if it were an old woman speaking.

'There isn't a single thought or idea that isn't soiled by a relationship like this,' she went on, 'and underneath all the beauty of life I see only wretchedness, it's sick – so nauseatingly sick! I can't touch anything without infecting it and I shudder as I do it. How often I've sat watching some old woman – such as my mother might have been, had she lived – and been wretched enough to see her grey hair and think with a kind of malicious pleasure: perhaps she's been no better than me. You see – fallen women are always brazen.'

She gave a harsh laugh. It gave her some relief to torment herself. She felt that her guilt was diminished by the fact that she was inflicting her own punishment.

'The old woman I presumed to offend in my thoughts might actually have been a decent wife, whose shoelaces I wasn't fit to tie,' she went on. Her voice wavered, and her eyes, still fixed on the same point, slowly filled with tears, 'Not like me, only decent on the outside – but a real wife who had given everything from love and for love – whose whole life had been one long endeavour for those who were dear to her ... for the children, of whom she was doubly fond, because they were his as well ... Ah, it's the harshest punishment imaginable, not being able to touch the purest of things without sullying them.'

She threw herself onto the chair, her face pressed into her arms as they rested on the window frame, and a long, moaning sob was heard. She had almost forgotten his presence and who she was talking to, so immersed was she in her own train of thought.

He felt sorry for her. Even though the cause was reduced in his eyes to a mere chimera, he did not doubt that her distress was genuine.

'Why torment yourself like this?' he said mildly.

She lifted her head, turned round without shifting her arms, and regarded him with mournful, tear-filled eyes.

'You, who are free, and can never be anything else, find it hard to imagine how it feels for someone who has renounced all rights to her own self, yet still knows herself to be a real, living person, a thinking being with her own will,' she said.

'How often you would come home from some dinner, flushed and excited after the wine! And you would stroke me under the chin in that way I've come to hate so much, because I knew you were going to lift up my face and kiss me. I sat there as dead and heavy as a lump of wood; and for that, too, you would reproach me! You had no idea what that alone cost me, no idea I was gritting my teeth to stop myself lunging out and biting anything within reach, like a wild horse. You had no idea what it meant to keep my composure, when seething inside me there was a frenzied urge to throw you to the ground and stamp on you! Yes, there were times when I was really afraid that in my madness I would do you violence.'

The words came raining down on him like blows, and it was impossible to doubt their veracity; there was proof enough just in her toneless voice, quivering with suppressed emotion. He felt himself enclosed in an invisible net which was implacably being drawn tighter around him.

'But I've done everything for you,' he said compliantly.

'Yes, yes,' she cried impatiently, painfully aware that she could not utter a word of the truth without offending him, yet determined to put an end to all dissimulation. 'That's not what I'm talking about. You've paid me handsomely – one might even say royally.'

She ran her hand down one of her sleeves, so the soft velvet of the dress moulded itself more closely to her firm arm. Against the deep black of the material, her hand seemed all the whiter – that large, strong hand which should have been toughened by life's labours, but which had been exempted from them by two plain, heavy rings.

'I'm not like other women any more,' she said sorrowfully. 'I *can't* value myself in money, whether the sum is small or great. It's abnormal, if you like – in fact it's simply ludicrous not to be able to cope as even the humblest do. But it's impossible – I can't do it any more.'

'What is it you want then?'

He had felt so secure in his possession, and now she was slipping, slipping; where would it end? He was seized by an ill-defined fear of losing her. For he did really love her – in *his* way – and he had spoken truly: he did think that she had 'grown into a fine woman'.

'I want to keep myself by working, that's all,' she said gently, as one might speak of a beautiful dream one hardly dares to

179

mention, for fear of seeing it dissolve on exposure to another's critical gaze.

'Keep yourself? What do you mean? I keep you, don't I?'

The Squire turned his head in all directions, at a loss where to spit.

'Yes. But I want to do it myself – I can't stand this any more.'

She shivered as she got up, and cast a furtive glance at the bottles of champagne.

'You've no right to refuse to fulfil your obligations; you're my wife in the sight of God and man.'

The Squire spat emphatically in the direction of the stove.

'Wife? Oh, what abuse of the word!' She stood facing him. Her cheeks had lost their colour, but she looked him boldly in the eye.

Now anger got the better of him and his indignation erupted.

'So-o, the old ties don't suit you any longer,' he let fly in his fury, biting on his cigar, leaving tobacco leaves shredded on his lips. 'The female craving for novelty! ... It's got to be some young Adonis ...'

She looked at him, stiffly and dismissively; and there was something in that cold gaze which held him back.

'There's no man in the world I would want to marry – now,' she said grimly, as if talking of an injustice done long ago.

'Oh well, so it's freedom you're hankering after,' he said. 'But absolute freedom doesn't exist. Every position in life brings with it some kind of constraint; poverty not least. Remember that the first group to revolt against the established order of things were the fallen angels. Satan, the fount of all evil, isn't stupid, he knows very well how to put his designs in the best light, and *freedom* is the word he uses to gild them most often. But evil is evil and right is right.'

The Squire had an unshakeable belief in his own powers of eloquence, but he was too easy-going to deploy them except in extraordinary circumstances like these. So when Selma merely made a dismissive gesture that indicated she was not convinced, he found himself utterly nonplussed. He thought his account had made matters absolutely clear. Could anyone really have any objection to the assertion that evil is evil and right is right? He began to suspect that his wife must be possessed by the Devil or something of the kind. Then he made a hasty mental review of all the bachelors he knew, but none of them seemed more of a threat than the rest. He detested them all equally. An unmarried man was to him an objectionable creature, a kind of vermin, now that he himself was married.

'Haven't you had freedom enough? You've been allowed to do anything you wanted! But it's all these Doll's House theories, it's the Devil and his ...'

'No it's *not* theories, it's my whole nature in revolt, it's nothing – *nothing* more or less than the fact that I can't bear to have your hands touching my body!'

She thought herself that her words sounded rather crude, and it drove the blood up to her temples, but the truth must out, once and for all, whether it sounded ill or well.

'Anyone who breaks the vows given at the altar puts himself beyond the pale, and how can a person live with that on their conscience?'

He felt sure he would fell her with his slogans, but she was tough-skinned.

'But as I've told you, the vow I gave as a child is not binding on me as a woman, whether it was made at the altar or anywhere else. Don't you see that that's the crucial point, where all the threads come together? The fact that no-one has the right to accept a lifelong vow, if the person making it isn't fully aware of its implications. How many women entered into marriage as I did? If the ties feel intolerable, may they break out of them as I am doing!'

She tossed back her head, her eyes glittering. The tone of her own words inspired her courage, and at that moment she felt that the whole world was open to her – that she need only 'break out', and then she would be free.

'You should be very careful, because you are not the only one concerned here,' he said menacingly. 'Every word of that kind is a flaming brand thrown out to wreak destruction. Man is woman's head – both divine law and human law tell us so – there must be firm rule in the state and the family. The state is founded solely on family life. He who overthrows the family, overthrows everything.'

'No-one puts a higher value on family life than I do,' she said firmly, 'but we have no family. Nor can there be anyone more convinced than I am of the sanctity of marriage. But if that is so, it mustn't be entered into as thoughtlessly as now, and above all not until the age of majority, when we are fully aware that we are responsible for our own actions, and that we have taken our own fate into our hands in earnest – and that we ourselves must take the blame and accept the consequences. If we haven't reached the point where we feel that, then we aren't mature enough to take such an important step as marriage should be. As far as you and I are concerned, nothing stands between us but my loathing, my unconquerable dread of your advances. I esteem you, I am even fond of you, but – at a certain distance. Children would undeniably have bound us together, but as it is, there are no children. This concerns only you and me. As a human being, I'm nothing to you – absolutely nothing. My thoughts and feelings are as alien to you as if I lived on the moon. If I could put my personality on one side and my body on the other, you wouldn't hesitate a moment over your decision. You're indifferent to what I suffer, as long as I belong to you and – keep quiet. *That's* what I can't forgive you!'

For a moment she had to fight back tears. Such a feeling of loneliness overwhelmed her, but she overcame it.

'If I had been a business associate, a companion, a friend,' she went on, 'then you would have missed me and said some kindly words of farewell. But I'm infinitely less than those, and so all you feel is anger at having been cheated in a transaction. Why worry about it? There are plenty of celebrated, beautiful, respected women, who'll gladly sell themselves for the price of a tidy fortune, if only the clergyman will put his seal of approval on the deal. Take one of them, and let me go.'

It was a strange feeling that these words produced in him, something ill-defined, like a longing for – he did not know what. It was so new and painful – no, he couldn't, *couldn't* do without her! He would say anything to convince her that it was impossible!

'Go?' he repeated. 'You're not considering what you're saying. You'll never endure the scandal ... the slander ... all those things you'll be laying yourself open to. I know you: you're far too proud to bear it. The shame of a step like that would crush you.'

'Shame only has any power over a person for as long as they give in to it. From the moment they defy it, it's nothing.'

With an overwhelming sensation of youthful strength, she leaned back and stretched out her arms, so her slender figure was outlined in the shape of a cross against the light curtain. It was a movement that instantly revealed the unconstrained beauty of her whole figure – not laced into a corset, but supported by nature's supple strength – a delicate litheness, giving the impression that it could be bent like coiled steel and spring back into place. The fork-tongued snake's head caught the light, sending out long, multi-coloured flashes.

He watched her in silence.

'Where is it you want to go?' he suddenly exclaimed. Fear of losing the initiative drove him to abandon oratory and resort to more concrete arguments. 'These are utopian dreams. There's no career for you, no future. Just think about it, and you'll see that what you've set your hopes on is impossible. You would quite simply not be able to provide for yourself, spoilt as you are by seven years of riches and refinement. You love money, or rather, everything that money can buy. Think how much your books alone cost! How could you live without all that ... all your interests ... everything you've grown so attached to? You won't have time to spare a thought for anything but the struggle for your daily bread. And what do you want to be? A clerk? You've never been trained in commerce. A teacher? You've knowledge, but no qualifications. A seamstress? You don't know how to cut cloth. And there would be scores of you fighting over every piece of bread.'

He waited, and said no more.

She had to bite her lip to suppress the complaint that was

trying to force its way out, and his words had deflated her. This was the very objection that had always raised itself within her, and therefore the one she feared most.

He noticed that he had the upper hand and, rolling the loose tobacco leaves more tightly round the tip of his cigar, resumed:

'A runaway wife is viewed with scorn by all decent people. They shun her as they would any other adventuress. You'll find yourself snubbed at every turn and, thrown out into the world defenceless at the age of twenty-three, who can say what temptations you might fall for.'

'I'm quite safe from one kind of those, at least,' she said, with one final attempt at brightness. But the sense of powerlessness already lay heavily on her.

Within her was a yearning to work, to be of service to others – to become wholly engrossed in it – but she was not so naive as to believe that a woman could achieve any more with her two bare hands than merely supporting herself. And she knew that she would never be satisfied with vegetating – with living only in order to earn her daily bread. What a life! Would she find herself sinking into that materialism, born of poverty, which had so often disgusted her in others? It was the hundredth time she had faced that question, and now it demanded an answer more insistently than ever before. She felt a trembling spasm, and had to clench her teeth to prevent them chattering.

'And who would offer you work?' he asked triumphantly, for she was pale, her eyes were cast down and there was something about the way she had slumped that told him she was giving up the fight. 'Lots of people want to work, but ... is there a single place that would take you on without recommendation, and who would recommend you? Me, perhaps?'

He gave a short laugh and rocked back in his chair, taking several puffs at his cigar, which he had almost finished. He felt sorry for her, in the same way as he did when he whipped his favourite horse; he felt simultaneously pleased about the beneficial effect it would have.

'Compelling arguments, aren't they?' he added, and his tone was positively genial.

'Yes,' she replied curtly, but her downcast eyes glinted with the creeping, bitter loathing of the oppressed. He had bent her to his will before, but each time it took greater effort, and he had only one means: money.

It was only now, at her defeat, that she realized she had unconsciously been nurturing the hope that he would extend a helping hand: ease her first steps and find her work. Now she was ashamed of that hope, as if it had been a crime. Yes, it was more than that: it was an absurdity. She could see that now, and a fiery blush went stealing across her cheeks once more. But she kept her eyes lowered, fixed on the carpet with shame.

She heard her husband moving about, preparing to go to bed; she observed him take one candle to his bedside table, the other to her own. He was still attentive. So everything would remain as it had been; he would never mention this conversation, and they would pretend that nothing had been said.

She felt so fettered that she could not leave the room, because out there in the night and the darkness were the gaping jaws of poverty and abandonment. She did not possess even the tiniest sum that she could call her own – earned by her labour.

If he had approached her at that moment, she would have been capable of strangling him with her bare hands, for she knew that he was right: no-one can spend seven years in a rich man's home and go unpunished.

But the Squire was of a sanguine disposition, was pleased with his victory, did not want to push his luck, and had high hopes of the next day.

When he had finished, he undressed and got into bed.

Before pulling the cover up over his ears, he cast his wife one last glance. She was still standing motionless, rooted to the spot, her head bent, and he saw the diamond eyes of the snake sparkling in the light as her breast rose and fell in panting breaths.

He could see that she was agitated, but she would be over it by the next day.

And he put out the candle.

She remained standing by the window, deep in thought. The

sparse light from her bedside table left the more distant parts of the room in dusky shadow.

Her pulse was beating wildly, and contradictory thoughts chased through her head like fantastic shadows in a torchlight procession as it passed.

She had sought the truth, within herself and beyond, in the way only they seek who know that their welfare depends on this one thing: finding their own conviction, for which they can both live and die.

She had read those publications which say that a life together with no content is not a marriage, even if it is sanctioned by a wedding ceremony. And she had read sharp attacks from the other side, claiming that form is everything, as long as it is held in respect.

Those were the theories. For her, they were not enough. She must find something so tangible that she could grasp it and say: this is mine. *Belief* was what she demanded, not belief that is acquiescent, but belief that is alive. She had imagined that she possessed such belief, but it was not hers, it came from books. That was why it was faltering now.

Bitterness engulfed her.

It is so easy to stand in one's room, shake another person by the shoulders and say: you have lost. And then, when he looks questioningly up into your face, to point out into the night and say: there lies your road! But the way? The way to find that road, when everything is equally dark?

That was what the theories had done, when she had begged them for something in which to place her trust. And now she knew that only life itself can give us that, and all the other things are pointers, but that no-one can live on another person's theories, only on their own belief.

The very things she had believed she felt most passionately for, the very things she had considered unshakeably certain, could scarcely survive being thrown out into cold reality or exposed to the light of critical scrutiny before they evaporated and were gone.

Gone? ... Was it possible then, that after all this she could acknowledge that man's claims to possession of her person?

The idea of suicide passed fleetingly through her mind. But her fit and healthy constitution, with all its aversion to death, revolted against it. She could always resort to *that* if everything else proved futile.

Did wealth mean everything to her then, everything? Was she one iota better than those alms-hungry creatures she had learnt to despise for their greed? Or was there any tie that bound her to this man, other than money?

That was what she wanted to discover.

Perhaps he himself would reject her, once she was no longer his passive possession – the form without the soul. He would be free to choose. Free? Oh, she knew him. There could be only one outcome.

She cleared a space on the table, where the supper was still laid, and took out her writing things.

Her initial enthusiasm had admittedly evaporated in the face of his interjections, of the spectre he had conjured up: poverty. But a calm, cold resolution remained.

She sat down and wrote:

Richard!

Look for a place for me at some institute of physical education down in Germany, and write as soon as you have found one. We need not meet, this can be arranged just as well by letter. You know what I have covered in my studies, and how I have persevered; you know they are too narrowly theoretical, but that can be rectified. I need say no more. You will understand the rest.

Your cousin
Selma

She put the letter into an envelope addressed to Elvira, and asked her to redirect it. Then she placed it under her pillow. Tomorrow she would send it off.

All the suspense was over. Now she felt calm, because she knew what she wanted.

She looked across to the other side of the room, where he lay sleeping soundly with his face turned to the wall, and there was no longer any hint of bitterness within her. It was the sensation of confronting a superior force that had momentarily kindled her hatred.

Her eyes sparkled with the courage to live, because now she had taken the step, come what may. Her whole being was suffused with the youthful vitality of an egoism which shouts: 'Make way, I must live!'

Then she bent down and blew out her candle, because she wanted to get undressed in the dark.

1884-85

Translator's Afterword

Victoria Benedictsson (1850-88) wrote under the male pseudonym Ernst Ahlgren although her real identity soon became known. At the time of her premature death, her published works comprised two collections of scenes from local life (so-called *folklivsberättelser*), two novels, and two plays, one co-written. This is an impressive total, considering that she was only active as a writer for some four years. She also left behind a large amount of unpublished work, and an extensive set of diaries.

Benedictsson was a leading member of the group of radical, naturalist writers of the 1880s known as 'Young Sweden', identified with the early phase of the so-called Modern Breakthrough in Scandinavian literature. Her life and work were rooted in the province of Skåne in the very south of Sweden, where innovative writers were taking their literary lead as much from Copenhagen as from Stockholm. Her first novel *Money* (original Swedish title *Pengar*), written in 1884-5, shared Young Sweden's predilection for 'novels of disillusion'. It was also a contribution to the topical marriage debate, breaking new ground by daring to discuss the psychological and physical consequences of sexual relations where one partner wields all the power. It has become a classic of Swedish literature and is still widely read today.

Money is Selma's story, and in her Benedictsson created a unique heroine, lively, self-critical and painfully honest. Selma is unconventional in an age of stultifying social convention, and strong enough to weather the criticism she attracts. Her status is undoubtedly that of a Swedish Madame Bovary or Nora, and Benedictsson indeed saw the story as her own interpretation of problems raised in Ibsen's *A Doll's House* in 1879. But the Selma preparing to leave at the end is unlike Nora in several critical respects: she has no children and, aware of the insecurity and poverty that may result from breaking free, she has tried to make practical plans for her future. We do not actually see her leave, but Benedictsson implies that it is bound to be a messy, complicated business. She herself longed to escape from an unsatisfactory marriage to a man many years her senior, but opted to stay with him and instead found a creative outlet in her writing. A long illness and a period when she was unable to walk gave her time for study and work.

Selma strides onto the first page of the novel with hands thrust into her overcoat pockets, a gangling, dreamily naive, comically dogmatic teenager. The reader then witnesses her development into a statuesque woman with everything that money can buy, but physically and mentally frustrated. The energy that surges in the young girl, captivating her portly suitor as she comes in cold and rosy-cheeked with her ice-skates slung over her shoulder, is suppressed and driven inward to create a mature Selma who sometimes feels that she is suffocating. Selma's strength and vitality are stressed again and again, with repeated reference to her throbbing pulse and the incessant nervous movement of her hands as a reminder of the life within her. Almost the last words in the novel are: 'Her whole being was suffused with the youthful vitality of an egoism that shouts: "Make way, I must live!"'

The young Selma, however, her mother dead and her frail father reduced to poverty by failed business ventures, loves pretty clothes and fine horses and is easily manipulated by her clergyman uncle into marriage at sixteen to a rich local squire. The Rector sees all the temporal advantages, and Benedictsson leaves us under no illusion that the marriage is anything other than a financial transaction: the buying and selling imagery is insistent, from the title page on. Selma knows she is a kept woman, and the knowledge does not get any easier as she grows ever more dependent for her sanity on the books and the horse acquired at her husband's expense. The author implies that the easy way out would be to find relief through yielding to the advances of her cousin Richard, sparring partner of her youth, who is physically attractive to Selma and her intellectual equal. Benedictsson however chooses to make Selma resist him and realize that the only solution is to quit the hollow respectability of her marriage, where she is in effect prostituting herself, and try to survive alone, supporting herself by her own work.

But with her artistic ambitions abandoned, where can Selma go? When she writes to Richard in the closing pages, 'Look for a place for me at some institute of physical education down in Germany', she is not only getting as far away from her husband as possible, but also probably hoping to train as a physiotherapist, a new profession and one which even women could enter, although training was not widely available in Sweden at the time. Benedictsson had come into contact with physiotherapists during treatment to her leg, and would have known that a strong, fit woman like Selma, with some study of human physiology behind her, would have at least some chance of success in such a career.

Selma's bold step in a new direction is wholly in keeping with her character as we come to know it in the novel. Benedictsson seems to relish portraying her as a strong-willed heroine who does not conform to stereotypes of behaviour or appearance. She cares nothing for propriety as a girl, refuses to be chaperoned, withdraws entirely from local social life when her husband criticizes her for dancing with other men, and vents her frustration with life by swinging from the door lintel in his absence.

Selma is no conventional beauty either, and several of the other characters voice the opinion that she is ugly in her youth, but her appearance is very striking, both as an excitable young tomboy with a white face and red lips – 'like a lovely winter fruit', as her uncle puts it – and as a woman, pale, tall and slim, habitually dressed in dark, tight-fitting costumes which accentuate her silhouette and peak of physical fitness, yet are reminiscent of mourning. While working on *Money*, Benedictsson – herself no beauty – wrote to her friend Axel Lundegård, '... I like ugly people. The others can be nice to look at, but insipid' (Ernst Ahlgren, *Samlade skrifter* [SS] III, 1919, p. 258). One cannot claim, however, that Benedictsson is engaged in some feminist-inspired project to make Selma's personality more important than her looks, for she is clearly fascinated by her heroine's appearance. Perhaps, however, she realized that her ideal of attractiveness was a rather personal one, and that was why she made Richard share it; he could then explain how Selma's thick, yellow fringe and almost sallow complexion could be beautiful simply because they were so quintessentially *her*. Furthermore, it is implicit in men's reaction to Selma that the author well understood how little sex appeal has to do with conventional notions of beauty. But it is not always easy for the translator to reconcile Benedictsson's vision with the need not to rouse the reader's sense of the ridiculous: what is one to do, for example, with Richard's admiration in Chapter 7 of skin that he calls 'frestande glanslöst som en skalad banan' (literally: enticingly dull, like a peeled banana)?

The emphasis throughout is on how *natural* Selma's looks are. Her love of fresh air and exercise and her lack of vanity are contrasted with the artifice of Richard's wife Elvira, who spends much time in front of the mirror, crimping her hair and applying powder, actions which Benedictsson implies are symptomatic of her pathetic anxiety to please her husband. The mature Selma interestingly does not object to the principle of pleasing the opposite sex, perhaps because she is consistently trying to attract Richard herself, although she long remains blind to her own motives. She knows that her 'natural' appearance gives her power over him, and she exploits this, as in her stage-managed ride to allow him a farewell glimpse of her in the saddle, tousled and exuberant.

There is something quite theatrical too in the lighting effects Benedictsson wrote into her novel. The use of light and dark in the novel is a topic that deserves further investigation, especially as it ties in with the theme of art; like Selma, Benedictsson had wanted to study painting, and her interest in the visual arts is apparent in both the opening chapter and the visit to the National Gallery in Stockholm in Chapter 9. When the spotlight of the narrative is on a character, usually Selma, Benedictsson often places that figure in a darkened room within a pool of lamplight.

The author even alludes directly to painting in one instance, when the Rector enters the room after Selma has agreed to marry Squire Kristersson, and sees the tableau: 'With the lighting of a Rembrandt, the glow of the lamp fell on her fair hair and the wilful lines of her profile; everything else remained in shadow.' Truly intimate conversations, however, often take place in half-light, as do the frank dialogue between Selma and Richard when she is lying on the sofa at her father's apartment, and her final confrontation with her husband. Research in the 1990s highlighted Benedictsson's use of this technique in a more extreme form in her posthumously published story 'Ur mörkret' (Out of the Darkness), revised and published after her death by her friend and literary executor Axel Lundegård. Nina, lying in the dark, delivers a bitter monologue on the curse of life as a woman, feeling able to speak out because she is disembodied, freed from the object status that she suffers as a female body in a patriarchal society. The darkness is the home of the unconscious, the mysterious, the utopian (see Christina Sjöblad and Ebba Witt-Brattström in *Nordisk Kvinnolitteraturhistoria*, II, 1993, p. 529-31). More recent research by Lisbeth Larsson, however, reveals that Lundegård made extensive revisions to the Benedictsson texts he published posthumously, revisions aimed at highlighting her own tragic story, from which he stood to profit because her personal papers were by then his to sell. (See Lisbeth Larsson, *Hennes döda kropp: Victoria Benedictssons arkiv och författarskap*. Svante Weyler Bokförlag, 2008.)

It is not only the lighting that is theatrical in *Money*: the whole structure is like that of a play, although it was never intended as one, but began life as a short story which Benedictsson then expanded. The individual chapters/scenes are free-standing and tautly written, with great emphasis on dialogue and in places little description other than 'stage directions' enabling the reader to visualize the characters and setting. We know from the author's diaries that she had a very keen ear for the dialogue she heard around her, and plays were of course a very popular medium for the so-called 'indignation literature' of the emerging feminist movement in the 1880s, but Benedictsson saw herself as a storyteller, and there is also evidence that she found some of the dramas of the time, even *A Doll's House*, too didactic, too programmatic. She preferred a lighter touch, and did not want to compromise her creative freedom.

Interesting insights into the process of writing *Money* are provided in Benedictsson's correspondence with Axel Lundegård, son of the local vicar and himself a writer. They read each other's manuscripts and a close working relationship evolved between them, leading to an unusually honest and open friendship. Benedictsson valued Lundegård's constructive criticism, and wondered in one letter how she had managed to produce her volume of short stories *Från Skåne* (From Skåne, 1884) without the benefit of their 'workshops' (*atelierkritik*). Their discussions enabled Benedictsson to refine her writing technique as she worked on *Money*. At one point, having written a very successful description of a woman's hand which Lundegård wanted to incorporate into one of his stories, she concluded that concentrating on one small and finite task with all one's senses produced the most powerful results. She therefore applied that method in subsequent chapters of her book, writing what she considered the most important scenes first and then fitting the action round them. In Chapter 5, for example, she tells Lundegård that she began by writing three scenes: Axel's conversation with Richard, Selma waking up after her wedding night, and Selma taking leave of her uncle (*SS* III, p. 251-56).

The crucial morning scene, which has to express Selma's shock and revulsion after being confronted with the physical realities of marriage, was the subject of a discussion with Lundegård, and one which reveals a great deal about the constraints under which a woman writer must operate in the 1880s, as well as more about Benedictsson's instinctive narrative touch. Commenting on a draft, Lundegård asked whether Selma's thoughts about the previous night would not have been more explicit, and accused her of prudishness. Benedictsson replied firmly that of course Selma thought more than is written, and this is indicated by the section break at this point; that a light touch here will give greater impact to her revelations of her feelings in the final confrontation with Paul; that her feelings are well expressed in the chill morning mood and the soiled veil 'so lovely yesterday'; and that though a male writer could say more, as a woman she could very easily face charges of indecency from conservative critics. Benedictsson conceived the masterly idea of using the story of King Lindworm, whose wife discovers that at night he turns into a 'scaly monster, so slithery and cold that his embrace made her writhe in agony', as a way of expressing Selma's repugnance, but she was not sure whether she dared to use it, and Lundegård had to urge her to do so.

Critics have sometimes claimed that the platonic outcome of Selma's attraction to Richard and her distaste for physical relationships are reflections of Benedictsson's own ambivalent feelings about the erotic sphere, but a close reading of *Money* reveals it to be in fact a sexually highly-charged novel, and one that dares to acknowledge women's sexual desire in spite of the strict moral climate of the time. Some of the scenes between Selma and Richard positively vibrate with sexual energy and Selma's physicality is a thread running through the novel, as we have seen in the descriptions of her movements and mannerisms. In this, *Money* invites comparisons with *The Awakening* by Benedictsson's American contemporary Kate Chopin (I am grateful here to Susan Bandy of Ohio State University, who made the link in a recent conference paper). The suppressed energy of her girlhood is still seething inside her. Keeping her boorish husband at bay with her implacable coolness, she seeks a new outlet for her desire for physical contact and exercise and finds it: in horseriding, or more precisely, in riding her handsome Prince. I have written further on this subject in '"She was hot and sweating, her horse matted and wet": Horse riding and female physical freedom in Victoria Benedictsson's *Pengar*' in *Love and Decadence: Essays on Scandinavian Literature, Letters and Drama in Honour of Professor Janet Garton.* Ed. C.Claire Thomson. Norvik Press, forthcoming 2011. A first version of the paper was originally commissioned for, and has now been published in Danish translation in, *Litterære fortællinger om idræt i Norden. Helte, erindringer og identitet.* (eds Vicki Bjerre and Susan J. Bandy, Aarhus Universitetsforlag, 2010.)

The image of Selma as a sweaty, breathless figure, physically aroused by the thrill of her morning ride, is an undeniably sexy one. Why else would some editions of the novel – the fourth, for example (Bonniers 1910) – have been bowdlerized, for want of a better word, by the cutting of the entire episode of Selma's breakneck ride to allow Richard to take that image with him as he leaves? A passage referring to the possibility of Selma and Richard going riding together has also been cut. Lundegård in his Afterword to the 1919 edition briefly lists what he terms the 'substantial discrepancies' found in some editions but passes no comment. In fact, the cutting of these two passages represents an expurgation of Benedictsson's characterization of Selma as a sexual being. The deleted passage in Chapter 9 culminates in a description with unmistakably erotic overtones: 'Her cheeks were patches of vivid red, making her brow and chin seem paler than ever; her nostrils flared with her heavy breathing, and beneath the thin lines of her eyebrows, her light eyes were full of spirit and zest for life. She was hot and sweating, her horse matted and wet, and her skirt spattered with yellow clay.' In Chapter 8, Richard is sulking because Selma does not think it prudent to be seen out riding with him. In the abridged version, Selma simply says that she would like to have his company and they would find it easy to talk. In the original, on the other hand, Selma vividly imagines Richard's presence at her side and her own physical reaction to the motion and the warmth of the horse's body. Editors around the turn of the century obviously felt that such passages might be considered too explicit.

The edition I have used in making this translation is Victoria Benedictsson (Ernst Ahlgren): *Från Skåne; Pengar*, in the selected works edited by Fredrik Böök (Bonniers, Stockholm, 1950). It is complete to the best of my knowledge, but I note that half a sentence has been lost mid-way through Chapter 4 from both this and the 1919 editions, though it is present in the 1910 edition. The words in brackets are missing: 'All because of that "Paul". She found it so "amusing" to use it (to the richest magnate in the neighbourhood, while for him it was) like a caress as it stole half shyly, half mischievously from her lips.'

Benedictsson is very much identified with her home province, and critics of various eras have tended to rate her naturalistic short stories of rural Skåne life as her highest literary achievement. *Money* is set largely in Skåne too, of course, but although the materialism of the village folk features in the plot of the early chapters, they and their landscape are not really important; Skåne is in essence just a backdrop to the events of Selma's life. Some facets of that life are undeniably autobiographical, such as the thwarted artistic ambitions and the unhappy marriage to an older man, but appraisals of Benedictsson's writing all too often allow it be overshadowed by the dramatic events of her own life. Although she made a happy home for her stepchildren, Benedictsson never established successful relationships with either her husband or her own daughter, and she attempted suicide several times. The money she earned from her writing gave her some independence, and she spent much of her last two years in literary circles in Copenhagen, where she had an affair with Georg Brandes, one of the leading figures of the Modern Breakthrough. It is said that her brittle self-confidence was shattered by his dismissal of her second novel *Fru Marianne* (Mistress Marianne, 1887), which she considered her most heartfelt work, as a 'ladies' novel', and this is offered as one theory to explain her final, successful suicide attempt.

Benedictsson is now seen as an enigmatic figure, partly because of the obscure circumstances surrounding her death. Lisbeth Larsson, however, shows persuasively in *Hennes döda kropp* that Benedictsson's life and work were subsequently subjected to a high degree of myth construction and revision by those in her immediate and less immediate circles. Strindberg, for example, was ghoulishly fascinated by Benedictsson's fate, parts of which he fictionalised in *Miss Julie*. Larsson suggests that it is far more productive for the reader of today to turn the focus back onto Benedictsson's own texts. Few people are better placed to do that than the translator.

I would like to thank Linda Schenck, John Death, Louise Vinge and Helena Forsås-Scott for reading and other help with the first edition of this translation in 1999. I also had access to an earlier translation of Chapter 10 of *Money* by Verne Moberg, which was published in the anthology *Scandinavian Women Writers*, ed. Ingrid Claréus (Greenwood Press, New York, 1989). I am grateful to Janet Garton for reading and commenting on this revised edition.

Sarah Death
December 2010

HENRY PARLAND

To Pieces

(translated by Dinah Cannell)

To Pieces is Henry Parland's (1908-1930) only novel, published posthumously after his death from scarlet fever. Ostensibly the story of an unhappy love affair, the book is an evocative reflection upon the Jazz Age in Prohibition Helsinki. Parland was profoundly influenced by Proust's *À la recherche du temps perdu*, and reveals his narrative through fragments of memory, drawing on his fascination with photography, cinema, jazz, fashion and advertisements. Parland was the product of a cosmopolitan age: his German-speaking Russian parents left St Petersburg to escape political turmoil, only to become caught up in Finland's own civil war – Parland first learned Swedish at the age of fourteen. To remove Parland from a bohemian and financially ruinous life in Helsinki, his parents sent him to Kaunas in Lithuania, where he absorbed the theories of the Russian Formalists. *To Pieces* became the focus of renewed interest following the publication of a definitive critical edition in 2005, and has since been published to great acclaim in German, French and Russian translation.

ISBN 9781870041874
UK £9.95
(Paperback, 120 pages)

SELMA LAGERLÖF

Lord Arne's Silver
(translated by Sarah Death)
ISBN 9781870041904
UK £9.95
(Paperback)

The Phantom Carriage
(translated by Peter Graves)
ISBN 9781870041911
UK £11.95
(Paperback)

The Löwensköld Ring
(translated by Linda Schenk)
ISBN 9781870041928
UK £9.95
(Paperback)

Selma Lagerlöf (1858-1940) quickly established herself as a major author of novels and short stories, and her work has been translated into close to 50 languages. Most of the translations into English were made soon after the publication of the original Swedish texts and have long been out of date. 'Lagerlöf in English' provides English-language readers with high-quality new translations of a selection of the Nobel Laureate's most important texts.

Coming up in June 2011

9 781870 041850